The Uncollected Stories by Edgar Wallace

Volume III

Richard Horatio Edgar Wallace was born on the 1st April 1875 in Greenwich, London. Leaving school at 12 because of truancy, by the age of fifteen he had experience; selling newspapers, as a worker in a rubber factory, as a shoe shop assistant, as a milk delivery boy and as a ship's cook.

By 1894 he was engaged but broke it off to join the Infantry being posted to South Africa. He also changed his name to Edgar Wallace which he took from Lew Wallace, the author of Ben-Hur.

In Cape Town in 1898 he met Rudyard Kipling and was inspired to begin writing. His first collection of ballads, The Mission that Failed! was enough of a success that in 1899 he paid his way out of the armed forces in order to turn to writing full time.

By 1904 he had completed his first thriller, The Four Just Men. Since nobody would publish it he resorted to setting up his own publishing company which he called Tallis Press.

In 1911 his Congolese stories were published in a collection called Sanders of the River, which became a bestseller. He also started his own racing papers, Bibury's and R. E. Walton's Weekly, eventually buying his own racehorses and losing thousands gambling. A life of exceptionally high income was also mirrored with exceptionally large spending and debts.

Wallace now began to take his career as a fiction writer more seriously, signing with Hodder and Stoughton in 1921. He was marketed as the 'King of Thrillers' and they gave him the trademark image of a trilby, a cigarette holder and a yellow Rolls Royce. He was truly prolific, capable not only of producing a 70,000 word novel in three days but of doing three novels in a row in such a manner. It was estimated that by 1928 one in four books being read was written by Wallace, for alongside his famous thrillers he wrote variously in other genres, including science fiction, non-fiction accounts of WWI which amounted to ten volumes and screen plays. Eventually he would reach the remarkable total of 170 novels, 18 stage plays and 957 short stories.

Wallace became chairman of the Press Club which to this day holds an annual Edgar Wallace Award, rewarding 'excellence in writing'.

Diagnosed with diabetes his health deteriorated and he soon entered a coma and died of his condition and double pneumonia on the 7th of February 1932 in North Maple Drive, Beverly Hills. He was buried near his home in England at Chalklands, Bourne End, in Buckinghamshire.

Index of Contents

When the Tsar Came

Peter Petervitch* lived in a little hut by the side of the railway. His hair was fair and his beard was golden, and he had tired blue eyes that were filled with the weariness which comes to the eyes of men who have far horizons to scan. He wore a red shirt which flapped in the wind, and topboots of soft leather, and in the winter he had a big sheepskin coat with the woolly part worn inside and a fur hat. He did not wear the fur hat except furtively, for it had fallen from an open window of the train, and it was unusually valuable.

The correct form of this name is "Pyótr Petróvich."

It marked the beginning of an ambition, the fur cap. Because it was very evident that if one fur cap could so fall, others also might be displaced by a puff of wind, or the accidental jogging of an elbow. And it might not be a fur cap, but a wallet filled with a hundred rouble notes, as—so legend said—such a wallet had fallen between Tomsk and Irkutsk.

It had been seen by an officer of the railway, and the signalman had derived little benefit therefrom.

Since the new well had been sunk at the back of the hut, however, no officer of the railway had ever come; once a week on a slow train there came an insulting clerk from Irkutsk to throw the weekly salary which Peter's post carried, and to demand when the old well would be bricked over—a task they had set the indolent Peter.

Peter Petervitch was in his hut drinking tea and eating his midday meal of black bread and sausage, when far away he heard the shriek of an engine.

He wiped his beard with his red shirt sleeve and took down the green flag which hung on two hooks under the lithograph of the Tsar.

He crossed himself before the gaudy little ikon near the door, and went out to do his duty.

The line was a straight ribbon of steel, stretching from cast to west. It crossed a flat and featureless desert, and there was nothing to obstruct the view from horizon to horizon.

Somewhere to the westward, where the two parallels of steel rail met in a quivering heat mist, he saw the black speck of the onrushing express. A verst* away a tiny figure of a man stood with a green flag before a little white hut—another atom of humanity.

Russian: верст, an obsolete unit of measurement equal to 3,500 feet or 1,067 meters)

Peter glanced eastward. Between his post and the next the line was clear. He unfolded his green flag and solemnly extended it.

The express went roaring past.

"Whr-r-r-r!"

There was one saloon of unusual colour and size.

It was pure white, magnificently proportioned, and the big windows were very big.

Peter saw a child by an open window. He caught a glimpse of her fair young face, saw, in a flash, the smile on her lips as she talked over her shoulder with an officer who stood behind her. Then the train was gone.

He looked long and earnestly at the disappearing rear carriage, its outlines obscured by the cloud of dust which chased it madly, refolded his flag and mechanically threw a glance along the side of the ballasted road.

There was no fur cap, no wallet—nothing.

Nothing? Peter walked slowly along the railside. He stooped and picked up a handkerchief.

It was a dainty affair, all lace and fine cambric, and as he turned it over with his big strong hands, there rose to his nostrils a faint and beautiful fragrance.

Peter sniffed at it, inhaled the delicate loveliness of it. There was a design worked in one corner. A design incomprehensible to Peter. It was a raised design, and had eagles and lions and swords, and such things.

Peter had seen handkerchiefs before, in the big stores at Irkutsk. But then you may see everything at Irkutsk because it is the most wonderful city in the world, and has electric light and beautiful churches, and people wear white shirts—even common people. But never before had he seen such a thing as this.

He was embarrassed more than a little with his find. A fur cap you may wear on holy days. A wallet full of hundred rouble notes can be spent at Irkutsk, though God knows a hundred roubles is a great deal of money, and would require some ingenuity to spend! But a spider-web of cambric, with edgings of something as unsubstantial as smoke. Peter shook his head in perplexity and carried the wonder into his cabin.

Beneath the ikon was a little niche where a candle may stand and did stand when candles were plentiful. Peter cleaned the niche of grease, placed the handkerchief in its place, made the sign of the cross twice, and said, "Christ have mercy!" Then he went back to his tea, his sausage and his thoughts. He was not a great thinker. His mind moved slowly—like one of those big-wheeled tarantass* that carry country people in summer-time, across the bad roads of Siberia. He was elementary and naturally indolent, the scope of his mentality was bound by the deeps of hunger and the supreme height to which a man rises who gets drunk on beer.

Russian: тарантас, a four-wheeled horse-drawn vehicle on a long longitudinal frame, reducing road jolting on long-distance travel. It was widely used in Russia in the first half of the 19th century. It generally carried four passengers. (Wikipedia).

Considering the matter for three days he came to the conclusion that the handkerchief was suitably employed as an object of offering.

Summer passed and the winter came, and with winter he wore two shubas,* a sheepskin hat, and the fingerless gloves which a paternal government supplied.

Russian: шуба, a fur coat.

Day by day he would stand in the biting blast to pass the trains eastward or westward, and six times a week he would search the line for the jettison of the Trans-Siberian express.

The winter went, the spring came, and Peter, shedding his shubas cautiously, came by easy stages to the red shirt and the soft leather boots of summer.

He had a brother, one Andrew, who had worked at Irkutsk for a skin merchant and earned seven roubles a week, which is about fourteen shillings, and is good pay. But Andrew was at once a source of sorrow and pride to the good Peter, for this town-haunting brother was a Socialist in his sluggish way, and did not believe in God. Else how could a man calmly relinquish so excellent a position as chief porter to a skin merchant and go wandering to the unknown cities of the west—to Moscow, even as far north as Riga?

From time to time letters came to Peter—bombastic letters. Andrew was prosperous. He wore white linen, and he had gone so far in his magnificence to promise that some day he would send Peter a five-rouble note. Beyond that he did not go.

Peter, saying his prayers before the little ikon, often prayed that the five-rouble note would come along, and when he had crossed himself he would touch the handkerchief for luck. The wisp of linen had grown somewhat grimy from overmuch touching, but the scent, which was peculiarly its very own, still clung about it when the adventure came to Peter.

He had just finished his frugal ablutions and had given "all clear" to a slow passenger train when he saw a fast tarantass being driven along the rough road which bordered the line. It was coming towards him, bumping and jolting over the uneven surface, and Peter took off his hat and quaked a little, fearing that this might be an official of the line.

The steaming horses were pulled up with a jerk a dozen yards from the cabin, and a gentleman stepped down.

He wore red boots up to his knees, and his clothes were of velveteen, and Peter, who knew he was no representative of Government because he was innocent of uniform, thought possibly that this was the millionaire who had lost the fur cap, and quaked again.

"Peter Petervitch!" roared the newcomer in a boisterous voice. "Come and kiss me, for I am your brother!"

And indeed it was!

Peter ran forward and took the man in his arms, kissing him on both cheeks, on the forehead and on the chin.

"God bless you!" said Peter. "You are a rich man, as I see. Now I am glad, for you will give me the five-rouble note which you promised me."

Andrew laughed again as the other led the way into the hut. He laughed long and readily, as a stoutish man with a red face will laugh.

"You shall have a sackful of five-rouble notes, my little brother," he said, patting Peter upon the back, "for I have come to make you rich."

They sat down together and ate. Though Peter had had one breakfast, he found no difficulty in eating another, for he had never eaten a satisfying meal in his economical life.

"Now," said Andrew as he dived into his pocket and produced a handful of cigarettes, "we will talk."

He smiled his cheerful contempt of his brother as Peter said his devotions to the ikon behind the door—those devotions which invariably follow every meal in the peasant's hut.

"Gospodi pomiluj!" sneered Andrew. "Lord have mercy on you! Whilst you pray, fat hogs feed on your richest food. I think you are a fool. What is that?"

He pointed to the soiled little handkerchief.

"That is a blessed object which came to me," said Peter gravely, "from a little child who had a face like an angel. It is scented with the incense of God."

Andrew clicked his lips impatiently, then he laughed.

"Sit down, O saint," he said ironically, "and I will give you incense which smells sweeter."

He thrust his hand into an inside pocket and drew forth a thick bunch of banknotes.

He laid them out on the table one by one, till they covered its surface. They were five-rouble notes, and there were many—so many that in places they lay two, one upon the other.

Peter gasped in silence at the display of wealth, and when Andrew stood on one side with the triumphant gesture of a showman. Petervitch came forward fearfully, touching the notes gingerly with his fingers.

"My brother," he said huskily, "praise be to God, for you are a rich man!"

Andrew looked at him as his fingers moved from note to note, and a little smile trembled at the corner of his mouth, for there was little more than five hundred roubles on the table, and Andrew had been given two thousand to accomplish the work.

He went to the door of the hut, opened it, and looked out. There was no soul in sight save the driver of the tarantass. He shut the door and came back into, the hut.

"Peter," he asked in a low voice, "do you ever think about Russia?"

Peter stroked his golden beard and looked at the other in astonishment.

"God save you, Andrew," he said in amazement, "why should I think about Russia?"

"Do you think of the devils who torture men and women?" asked Andrew, with simulated ferocity, for Peter did not inspire the natural zealous flow of wrath which is rightly the accompaniment to such a proposition as he had to make.

"I have heard of the domovýe,"* Peter answered dubiously, "and also of the rusálki,** those beautiful maidens who wait by the lakes and tickle girls to death, also the vedni*** who milk cows."

Russian: домовые, pl., spirits of the hearth, brownie-like fairies.
**Russian: русалки pl., spirits of the rivers and lakes.*
***vedni (sic). Wallace may have meant vodyány (Russian: водяный), the fairy king of waterways, or, perhaps ved'mý (Russian: ведьмы), witches.*

"You are a fool, Peter," said his brother, struggling to preserve a straight face. He could not afford to laugh in view of the seriousness of his mission. "You are just a brute fool, Peter," he went on vigorously, "as thousands of others of your kind are—content to sit and suffer and watch these other and stronger brutes trample over you, and oppress your women and your children."

"God save you!" gasped Peter in consternation. "He who told you I had a woman or children has lied!"

Andrew wrung his hands helplessly.

"What can I do with this fool?" he muttered. Then: "I am not speaking of you," he said, "but of the men you know. Listen to me. Would you like your brother to be a happy man?"

"You know that I would, Andrew," said Peter, "so why do you ask?"

"Would you like yourself to be rich and to ride in fine carriages and to wear cloth coats and sleep in beds with sheets?" Peter had no desire to sleep in beds with sheets; he had once tried the experiment in a reckless moment, and had never ceased to regret the chill contracted on that occasion.

But his brother went on:

"We are near Heaven, Peter. In a few months Russia will be free of the yoke which is round her neck. We will terrify these masters of ours so that they will give us what we ask. And you"—he slapped the other on the shoulder with his heavy hand, and stepped back with a look of admiration upon his face—"you shall free us!"

"I shall free you?" said Peter in bewilderment. "Now you are talking madness, my brother. I know nothing of what you mean. How can I help you—you who are so rich and have so many friends?"

"Sit down." Andrew caught him by the arm and dragged him to a stove by his side.

He spoke concisely and earnestly, and Peter listened; at first uncomprehending the trend of the other's speech. Then, as it slowly dawned upon his dull mind, he rose with a gasp of horror, and his face went white.

"What!" he stammered. "Wreck the train of our holy master! Andrew, you are mad."

"Don't shout!" hissed the other. "Do you want the whole of the world to know what we are talking about? You have got to do it, do you hear? If you don't I shall lose my life. I have sworn to my society to carry out its orders, and if I fail my comrades will kill me. You have to decide whether the life of your own brother or the life of the Tsar is more precious to you. To-morrow there will come news to you that the imperial train is going to Tomsk. The Tsar remains for the great festival and then returns. Nothing is to be done until the return journey. I will arrange everything, Peter; you need do no more than wave your green flag. I will have a fast tarantass ready to take you off, and you shall be kept in a small village until the matter is forgotten."

It was an airy proposition that Andrew Petervitch put before his brother—condemning him to death as he did knowingly and without remorse, that he himself might benefit to the extent of a few thousand roubles. Peter's detection was sure. Andrew himself might reasonably hope to escape in the confusion, if indeed he had not prepared a way for himself before the catastrophe. A few sticks of dynamite on the line could be carefully timed, might even be fired from a safe distance; the slow-willed Peter could either fly or wait and take his chance.

Peter listened as the plan was unfolded—listened with bulging eyes and ashen cheek, hypnotised by the plausibility of the other, scarcely understanding one half that was said save that he was called upon to commit a deed which was more dreadful than Peter in his wildest moments had imagined. He had thought at times, when the dull monotony of his life had driven him to mild desperation, of terrible crimes which he might commit, such as striking the clerk of the Irkutsk Station who was so rude to him, or making faces at the occupants of the slow-moving passenger trains, or even—the very thought left him breathless!—of setting fire to his hut one deadly day when the monotony of his loneliness had almost driven him mad.

"What is one life?" argued Andrew. "And what is one man's life more than another?" He did not explain by what miracle the outrage would destroy only the life he sought. "Some day there will come to you the knowledge—the great knowledge that the killing of a man is nothing!" He waved his large hands in contempt. "That day will come soon, and you will only be proud of your work."

Peter listened in silence to his brother's hearty farewell, and watched the tarantass as it jerked its way over the lumpy road to the distant flat line of the horizon. Then he went back to his hut and prayed. He made no reference in his prayers to the awful proposal which had been made; he felt it was not a moment to take God into his confidence until he himself had a clear idea as to what it was all about, and his fingers rested a little longer upon the cambric in the niche. He strove with greater earnestness, holding the little gossamer near his nose to catch the perfume. Then he went back to his work at the well—work he hated because it was unjust that he, a signalman, should be called upon to perform the labour of other and higher paid men.

All night long he lay awake thinking.

At dawn there came a light engine carrying an official of the line even as Andrew had predicted. A loud-mouthed, noisy, bullying official, none other than that objectionable clerk from Irkutsk Station, who gave him certain instructions about a mysterious train which would pass at noon. It was a train of the highest and the greatest importance, this much the clerk impressed upon him, calling him pig and fool, and little bear to point out the importance. And Peter listened, nodding his head, and the engine went speeding down the section to the next section-house, where it halted to repeat the instructions.

Peter was more than ordinarily careful with his ablutions that morning; he washed himself with great thoroughness, and took from the little box beneath his bed a blue blouse, washed and rough dried, but of a more brilliant blue than any of its fellows. He even combed his beard, and used the broken-toothed instrument to bring some kind of order to his tangled hair. One thing was certain, the Tsar was coming— that great and God-like man, his master and the master of all the world by Peter's reckoning, for he took no notice of the lies which were told, doubtless by interested people, that outside of Russia existed other territories dominated by other and less luminous Tsars.

As the hour got nearer he became more and more agitated. The day was a blazing one, the heat stifling and overpowering. Everything he touched that had been exposed to the sunlight was blisteringly hot, the whole landscape shimmered in a heat mist, and on the far horizon a dazzled brown mirage offered the illusory promise of shady trees and cool lakes.

Sometimes during a period of exceptional heat the sun would expand the rails to such an extent as to throw them out of the true. It was part of Peter's duty to make a careful examination half-way as far as the next section-house once a day.

An hour before the Imperial special was due he walked along in the scorching sunlight, his eyes fixed solemnly upon the twin grey rails. There had been an expansion; you could not put an edge of paper between the place where rail met rail. He had walked two hundred yards when he stopped. It seemed even to his unobservant eye that there was a distinct warp in one line. For the purpose of making his rough calculation he carried a piece of knotted string in his pocket, and with this clumsy apparatus he took laborious measurements and gasped.

For the first time since he had been in the employ of the railway company he had made a discovery which carried with it a reward of five roubles. Yes, here it was, two inches out of the true in one place— almost three inches in another!

He crammed his string in his pocket and went running back along the permanent way to his hut. He was distracted; he could not think what was the right thing to be done under the circumstances.

All that he knew was that the Tsar was coming in his wonderful train, and that he must be there at his hut to signal him past. But now? It never occurred to him, strangely enough, that the bulging rail was quite sufficient to throw the train off the line and bring the disaster by accident which his brother had planned should come through design.

He started walking to the next section to warn Ivan Menshikoff, the signaller. Then, in a panic, he realised that Imperial trains are notoriously unpunctual, and that bullying, brow-beating clerks from the Irkutsk Station might tell him a lie purposely deceiving him for the better safety of the Tsar. With this in his mind he ran hastily back to his hut, an uncomfortable figure, his face wet with perspiration. It was fortunate that his brother had not visited him that morning, and that he had nothing to distract him from his duty.

Then his heart suddenly came into his mouth. Far away on the west horizon was a blur of smoke. There would be no whistling, since this was a special train. The blob of dun-coloured smoke was all the warning an alert signaller required. He went hurriedly into his hut and came out again with his red flag. Of course, this was the proper course. It was a source of satisfaction that he had thought out this duty of arresting the progress of the Imperial special.

He lifted his flag, the flag that he had never had to use since the day of his appointment, unrolled it proudly, and stood at the door. He was probably the only signalman on the line that had had to show the red flag to the Imperial special.

Nearer and nearer came the train. A fear assailed Peter that the driver would not see him, and he waved the red flag frantically at a time when the driver could not possibly have seen him without the aid of a telescope. Nearer and nearer it came, and then with a sudden grinding of brakes the Imperial train jarred to a standstill, the engine less than fifty yards from the danger point, the great white saloon immediately opposite Peter's hut.

He stood there, his fur hat clutched in his hand, looking humbly, almost devotedly at the spotless car. He saw faces at the window and then he gasped, for one of the faces was that of a girl—the girl whom he had seen on the day he found the handkerchief. He had no time to speculate on this matter, for a uniformed officer, springing down the steps of the saloon, ran towards him.

"What is wrong?" he asked curtly.

Peter tried to speak, but could find no words, he was overcome at this tremendous moment.

"Speak, fool!" said the man.

"Gently, general!" said a voice.

The officer swung round with his hand at the salute, and stood rigidly facing the open window, which had been noiselessly lowered.

Peter looked up and saw a good-natured man with a little peaked beard, who turned his smiling eyes to the signalman.

"What is wrong, my friend?" he asked.

"Little father," stammered Peter, "the sun has opened the rails. God forgive me for delaying the holy Tsar, but when the rails are open I must stop the train, and if your excellency looks upon the face of the Tsar let him know that I did this because it is my duty."

It was a very long speech for Peter.

The kindly eyes were not moved from his.

"I am the Tsar," he said simply.

"God have mercy on us!" gasped Peter, and fell on his knees.

He was still dazed when the little party descended from the saloon whilst mechanics were putting the rails straight—not a matter that required any great waste of time—dazed when the Tsar and the beautiful girl walked along the permanent way and stood before his hut.

"And do you live here always?" asked the Tsar.

Peter nodded; he had no words.

The Tsar slipped into the hut and looked round.

"It is very clean," he said, as indeed it was, for Peter's usual shyness of soap and water did not extend to his habitation.

"What is this?" asked the Tsar in surprise. He crossed himself before the ikon as Peter might have done, and, reaching out his hand, touched the little handkerchief. He lifted it from its niche and examined it curiously.

"Why," he said, "this is yours, Vera."

The girl took it with a little frown of surprise.

"Yes, that is mine, papa," she said. "Look, there is my crest." She pointed to the embroidery in the corner.

"I found it!" blurted out Peter in terror. "Little father, it was by the side of the line, and I did not know that I was doing wrong, but it seemed so beautiful a thing that I placed it here and said nothing to any man, worshipping it because of the angel who had dropped it."

The Tsar threw back his head with a laugh, and turned to the officer behind him.

"See that this man receives a thousand roubles," he said shortly. "And he may keep the handkerchief, may he not?"

The girl smiled on Peter, and handed the precious relic into his hands.

Five minutes later Peter Petervitch stood, a confused and wondering man watching the disappearing train.

He with his own hand had touched the Tsar, had felt the warm grip of his fingers in a handshake. It was unthinkable, unbelievable! He was still in his maze when his jovial brother came, this time on a bicycle, for he wanted no evidence to accumulate against him.

The bicycle was a strange machine to Peter. He regarded it with a frown as partaking in some degree of his brother's revolutionary character.

Peter was engaged for the moment in drawing water from the new well—the well which had been sunk by the Government for his use—in order to mix the mortar with which to cover the old condemned well from whence he had drawn his supplies and from which incidentally his hapless predecessor on the section had met his death in the form of typhoid fever. Peter was in his red shirt, perspiring but immensely happy, singing in his great unmusical voice nothing more modern than an old folk-song he had learned at school.

Andrew dismounted from his bicycle and clapped the other on the shoulder. They kissed one another solemnly.

"Now come to the hut," said Andrew, "and tell me all your thoughts, my brother."

"I have no thoughts," said Peter meekly. "But many wonderful things have happened."

The other frowned. He looked round; there was no one in sight. Even the signalmen in the distant huts had retired to their midday meal.

"Tell me, Peter Petervitch," he said, "that you will do what I ask and make me a happy man."

"What do you ask?" asked the other.

"That you let me lay a mine on the rail." The other put it bluntly. "That is all. That you do not fire your gun or make an alarm, and that you go before the train comes."

"I will not do this thing," said Peter simply.

He was standing by the old well and, lifting a lump of stone, he dropped it over the edge, and stood listening until a faint splash below told that it had reached the water. He was more interested in his work than his brother apparently, and the red-faced man grew almost purple in his rage.

"Listen," he shouted. "Do you wish to see your brother dead or the Tsar dead?"

"I would rather see you dead," said Peter calmly after a moment's thought. And, stooping, he mixed water and lime with his curious bowl-shaped trowel.

Andrew looked at the man and a slow, cunning smile dawned on his face.

"If you do not help you are ruined," he said, "for I will go away and denounce you to the police."

That was a contingency upon which Peter had not speculated. To the police! And the news would go to the Tsar, and perhaps the little lady would want her handkerchief back from so unworthy a servant, who had listened to schemes for the destruction of her father.

He went pale at the thought. That he would also lose a thousand roubles did not distress him, because a thousand roubles was beyond his immediate comprehension.

"You will do this?" he stammered.

"Assuredly," said the other heartily. "Now which do you choose—my death or the Tsar's? Come, little brother, has not the day dawned when you see life as nothing?"

With surprising quickness for a man so lethargic Peter's hand shot out. A steel-like grip grasped the city-wasted Andrew by the throat and flung him round.

"Your death, my brother," murmured Peter, "go with God!"

He threw his weight forward, and, exercising the whole of his strength, he lifted the man bodily and flung him over the black edge of the well.

A despairing shriek came up as the man fell; a pause and a splash of water, and then silence.

Peter walked slowly to where the bicycle lay upon the ground, picked it up gingerly, and threw it down after the man. Then he went to work mixing mortar and carrying stones to cover over this place of death. And all the time he worked he whistled a tuneless song, for the possibilities of a thousand roubles was only at that moment dawning in his sluggish brain.

While the Passengers Slept

The dismal clang of the bell came plainly enough to Jordan's ears, and he leant over the side of the bridge and peered into the black waters. It seemed quite close, otherwise Jordan would not have looked, but to-night there was a thin, white haze on the sea.

He was one of the five men on the bridge of the Orthanic—five men heavily overcoated and muffled, for the night was bitterly cold. Captain Manson, a cigar clenched between his teeth, his hands in his overcoat pockets, stood close to the rail. Burton, the 'second', in the snug of the canvas screen, peeked vainly through his night glasses; a quartermaster, wheel in hand, showed dimly in the binnacle light, and there was a hint of another figure at the telegraph. Jordan was nervous and jumpy, all on edge, and small blame to him; he was a good seaman, and good seamen are superstitious, and the Carponic had gone down in these waters, as a warning to all optimistic ship officers who relaxed their vigilance in the English Channel. Not that the Carponic had been lax...

'Toll—toll!'

The sad, harsh clash of the bell came to him again, and he turned:

'You heard it, sir?' he asked fretfully.

The skipper grunted over his cigar.

'Yes—a wreck-buoy probably.'

'A wreck-buoy, sir,' repeated Jordan with polite scorn, 'in forty fathoms of water? There's no chance of a wreck fouling the shipping here. No, that's Calderwood's buoy.' He said this with grim decision, and the second officer shuddered behind the wind-screen.

'You give me the creeps, Jordan!'

Captain Manson chuckled.

'What a superstitious devil you are, Jordan!' he said, with a note of admiration in his voice, as though superstition was a rare gift, to be appreciated.

Jordan implicitly believed, and was not alone in his faith, that a wealthy syndicate existed in London which insured ships and employed men to cast them away.

'This is the twentieth century, Jordan. Things don't happen like that nowadays,' said the captain complacently.

'Human nature doesn't change,' growled the other.

'And you really believe that poor Calderwood puts a ghostly buoy in the water to warn mariners of danger!' Captain Manson laughed, and turned his kindly eyes upon the stolid figure of his chief officer. 'You ought to write a story about it,' he said drily.

'Pilot boat right ahead, sir!'

The vigilant Burton's voice split the conversation, and Captain Manson jerked an order over his shoulder. 'Stop her.'

The distant jingle of the engine-room bell and the answering clang were followed by a sudden cessation of sound as the pounding engines came to a rest.

'I know what I know, sir,' insisted Jordan doggedly. 'Calderwood and I were old friends. I don't believe his death was the result of an accident. I've heard that bell before—every seaman in this water has heard it in foggy weather.'

'If it wasn't an accident it was murder,' said the captain sharply—for him. 'You mustn't say that—very likely the man you accuse is coming on board in a minute.'

'Yes, I've a horrible feeling that he is,' said the other in a low voice. He was nervous and worried, all jarred and jangled with a fear which he could not analyse. It had been a hard crossing. Two days of fog across the Banks with meandering and vagrant ice-floes to increase the difficulties of navigation, and now fog again. The skipper realised something of the strain the man had endured, and dropped his big hand on the other's shoulder.

'Come, come, you mustn't let your prejudices run away with you,' he said kindly. 'Calderwood was a fine pilot—the best ever—I grant you that; but Grimwald, his mate, isn't a bad chap—a bit dour, but a good pilot.'

'He was on the Carberry Queen when she went down,' said Jordan.

'In a fog,' snapped the skipper; 'going dead slow. She ran into a barque—you can't make him responsible for that.'

'Pilot boat coming alongside, sir.'

The dancing masthead light of the pilot came under the starboard bow of the steamer.

'Slow astern,' said the captain, and the telegraph bell repeated his order. 'Take my tip,' he said, addressing the first. 'I'm an older man than you; get these ideas about ghosts and warning bells, and—bogies and things out of your head. It's not good for a young man to think like that—it's unhealthy.'

'Perhaps it is, sir.' Jordan walked to the side and looked over. The pilot cutter was fast, and a dark figure was reaching up for the ladder.

'Will he make it?'

'He's got it, sir.' He was impatient of delay at the best of times; now he lifted his megaphone.

'Stow that monkey ladder... What 'n thunder are you doing? All clear?'

'Ay, ay, sir!' shouted a distant voice.

'Cast off there, pilot cutter. Cast off, curse you! Are you deaf?' He turned with his hand at his cap. 'Pilot aboard, sir.'

'Full ahead!'

The telegraph bell jingled and the 'thump, thump' of the engines shook the bridge deck.

The deep voice of the quartermaster from the fo'c'sle hailed the bridge.

'Fog lifting, sir.'

'It was only a patch,' nodded the skipper. 'You ought to pick up the land as soon as she shifts.'

'Start light on the port bow, sir,' reported Burton.

He turned to the companionway. An awkward shape of a man was climbing up to the bridge. A big man, revealed by the bulkhead light, which he must needs pass in climbing, as one whose shapelesness did not end at a certain uncouthness of figure. The big, white face was unevenly assembled. The nose was crooked and the mouth twisted. His deep-set eyes burnt fiercely like a man consumed by an internal fever. All this Jordan saw looking down at the man with frank antagonism. Then he turned to the captain as the newcomer came to the bridge.

'Pilot, sir,' he reported.

'Come aboard, sir,' growled the pilot.

'Ah, pilot! Nice night.' The skipper nodded a smiling welcome.

'Nice enough,' said the other shortly. He looked at the binnacle.

'Strong tide running?' asked the captain.

'Bit of a tide—always is at this time of the year.'

'I suppose so.' He blew his whistle, and the pilot started suddenly. There were evidently two nervous men on the bridge that night. 'Get the pilot some cocoa,' he said to the quartermaster, who had come at the signal. 'Nervous, pilot?'

'I don't know about being nervous,' said the man gruffly. 'Sitting out in that pilot boat for four hours makes you a bit jumpy.'

Captain Manson nodded.

'So poor Calderwood used to say. You remember Calderwood?'

'Yes.'

'Lost his life in your boat, didn't he?' asked the chief officer carelessly.

'I remember'—Captain Manson was in his reminiscent mood—'you were coming out to pilot the Carponic. He was bringing her to Dover, and you were taking her up the river and you smashed into a sailing vessel that carried no lights—and you went down.'

'That's it. It wasn't my fault!'

There was almost a challenge in the pilot's voice, and the skipper laughed.'

'Not your fault! Of course it wasn't, pilot. Both ships were sunk. How did you get away?'

'I grabbed a lifebelt and swam for it,' said the man laconically.

'You were lucky,' Jordan broke in. 'It cost the underwriters a pretty penny. They said a lot of funny things, too.'

The man turned upon him fiercely.

'What do I care what they said! I did my duty. That's enough for me. They said somebody had insured cargo that wasn't on board, and that somebody made a quarter of a million through that barque gettin' in the way of the Carponic.'

'Without lights,' said Jordan significantly. 'Nobody ever discovered what ship she was. None of her crew were ever picked up. It wouldn't be a bad dodge for some scoundrel to abandon a ship at a certain point—a nice iron ship,' he said slowly, 'anchor her in the track of a steamer, and insure the unfortunate devil that struck her—What?'

The captain was going into the chart-room, but he stopped.

'Ah, but the pilot would have to know all about that,' he smiled. 'You could only do that if you could square the pilot. But you couldn't square the pilot. See?'

Grimwald thrust his big face almost into that of the first officer. Jordan did not flinch. In the half darkness of the bridge he stared into the eyes of the pilot, and after a moment George Grimwald turned with a growl in his throat to the man at the wheel.

'Half a point east, quartermaster,' he said.

'Why?' asked Jordan.

'I am piloting this ship,' snarled the other.

'I only asked out of curiosity.'

'Strong tides, I tell you.'

'But the tide should be running south now,' persisted Jordan.

'There's a bad current round here.'

What else he might have said in his rage was checked by the sing-song report of the look-out man on the fo'c'sle. The pilot stared ahead.

'Steamer on the starboard bow, sir.'

'Coasting boat,' he said gruffly.

The quartermaster brought him his cocoa. He would much rather have had a nip of whisky, and said as much.

'Not on this ship,' Jordan replied shortly. 'We're rather a nervous lot of people. When you're carrying six hundred human souls you can't take risks.'

Jordan walked across the bridge to where the second cuddled up to the wind-screen.

'What glasses have you got?' he asked.

'My own. What's the matter with 'em?' answered the other resentfully.

'Nothing. But use mine; they're much better for night work.'

Grimwald eyed the two men anxiously. All things were significant to him that night. People who gathered to speak in low tones were talking about him. What else could they discuss? He showed his yellow teeth in a contorted smile. Then he glanced at the man at the wheel.

'Quartermaster'—he dropped his voice so that it should not carry—'what are they whispering about?'

The wheelman spat thoughtfully on the grating.

'Nothing as I know of, sir.'

They were talking about him. They blamed him for the wreck of the Carponic. Curse them!

'You knew my mate Calderwood, didn't you?'

'Yes, sir. A nice young man he was.'

Grimwald nodded.

'Fell overboard out of my boat. Only him and me in it. Do you think that looked suspicious?'

He asked the question eagerly, and the unimaginative seaman gasped.

'Lor' bless your life, no, sir!' he said.

'People might say that I was trying to make him do something he didn't want to do, and that I got scared when he refused and shot him. They would say that, would they? Look!'

The quartermaster looked down, and nearly jumped. In Grimwald's hand was a long, black-barrelled revolver, and the nervous hands of the big man trembled at the trigger.

'Shot him with this,' he whispered hoarsely, 'that's what they'll be saying next. They put it about that I'm a rich man, that I grew rich suddenly after the Carponic was wrecked. But that's a lie. I had money left me, quartermaster, by an uncle in America. See?'

'I think you're worrying yourself about nothing,' soothed the seaman politely.

'Put her another point east.' He looked furtively at a little chart which he had taken from his pocket. 'Yes, a point. Calderwood fell out of my boat—accidentally.'

Jordan turned suddenly.

'You've shifted her course again, pilot,' he said sharply.

Grimwald nodded.

'There's a fishing fleet right ahead,' he answered.

Two pairs of glasses examined the sea.

'By Jove, you've got good eyesight!' said Burton. 'I can just see 'em.'

'I gotter have good eyesight,' growled the man. 'I don't believe in these glasses. Let me have a look.'

He took the binoculars in his hand, fumbled with them a moment, then let them fall with a crash to the ground.

'Be careful!' Jordan picked up his pet glasses with a curse.

'I haven't broken 'em?' asked Grimwald slowly.

'The chief officer swore softly as he examined his damaged glasses. Then he crossed to the little battery of speaking-tubes by the glass screen of his observation house.

'That the captain?' he asked, when an answering whistle shrilled. 'Jordan speaking, sir! Yes, everything all right; but I'm leaving the bridge for a moment to find my other glasses. Ay, ay, sir! Watch like the devil, Burton!' he muttered, as he passed his subordinate.

The pilot's eyes followed him, striving, as it seemed, to pierce the darkness which swallowed his antagonist—for such he knew him to be. Then he turned again to the binnacle with a shrug of his shoulders. He slipped a flat flask from his pocket, half-raised it to his lips; then, catching the steersman's eye, he extended his arm.

'Have a drink?' he whispered.

'No, thank you, sir; not on duty!' he said stiffly.

'Well, there's more for me!' growled the other; and strolled across to Burton. 'We've passed that fishing fleet?'

Burton nodded. He was peering anxiously ahead. The stars which had been hanging on the horizon were blotted out again.

Jordan came back to the deck with a second pair of binoculars, and so they stood for ten minutes, none speaking, staring ahead at the slow-heaving sea; and little by little, the belt of darkness on the horizon rose like a curtain.'

'Looks like a fog-bank right ahead,' said Burton suddenly.

'It's nothing; you get these patches in the Channel. We shall be through it in five minutes,' said Grimwald.

Jordan crossed again to his protecting screen and pressed a little bell. He walked briskly over to the port telegraph, and laid his hand on the lever.

'You're not going to reduce speed?' growled Grimwald.

'I am.'

'For a bit of smoke?' sneered the other.

'For a bit of smoke,' repeated Jordan; and rang the engines to half-speed. 'There are six hundred people on board this ship, pilot, and a very valuable cargo.'

'I'm in charge of this ship!' said the pilot loudly.

'You can tell us the way'—Jordan was brusque to the point of rudeness—'but I will decide how fast we go!'

The skipper, summoned by the bell, came up the companion- way buttoning his great-coat.

Jordan turned.

'Fog ahead, sir! I've reduced her to a half.'

Captain Manson clicked his lips impatiently.

'You're right! In a minute we shan't see the foc's'le!'

Through the patchy mist ahead came the melancholy boom of a siren. He turned with a little smile to the pilot.

'This is the kind of weather when I liked to have your poor friend Calderwood on my bridge. Slow ahead!'

A signal had brought the quartermasters to their stations.

Obedient to the command, the telegraph rattled over, and the clang of the answering bell came before a slower thud of engines told of the reduced speed.

The fog came with a rush. A grey cloud rose under the bows and swept over the foc's?le head, a swirling, wreathing blanket of wet smoke that hid even the foc's'le lights from view. Then of a sudden all the bulkhead lights went off, and the bridge was in absolute darkness.

'Who put out those bulkhead lights? Quartermaster, what the devil is the matter with the lights?'

'Fuse gone, I think sir,' said a muffled voice.

'Dead slow!' It was the captain's voice, and again the telegraph clanged.

'Calderwood, Calderwood—always Calderwood!' muttered Grimwald. Can't they talk of something else? Calderwood could see; Calderwood would pilot with his cursed eyes shut! But Calderwood is dead—dead—dead!'

He was speaking to himself, aloud. He was oblivious of the fog, forgetful of all else save that he could not get away from Calderwood—could not forget the face of the man, the despairing eyes of him as he went swirling to death in the wake of the pilot-boat, the waters all dull-red with his blood. Thus Grimwald had watched him, as he stood pistol in hand, hypnotised.

'Barque right ahead!'

The voice was at Grimwald's elbow.

'Who is that?' he gasped; and, as he asked, he knew.

His hair went up; he could feel his face shrivel and pucker with fear. He wanted to scream, and opened his mouth; but no sound came.

Then he saw.

Faintly in the fog the ghostly figure of a man by the quartermaster's side.

Calderwood!

Calderwood, white of face and horribly wet, little strips of seaweed hanging from his dripping clothes. Slowly the figure turned its head, and the mouth fell pitiably.

'Don't shoot me, Grimwald!' it whined. 'I've a young wife and a child! Don't shoot me, Grimwald! I can't wreck a ship; I can't do it! A point to the north!'

This last to the steersman, and the wheel went round slowly.

'Ay, ay, sir!'

The quartermaster answered mechanically, his eyes fixed on the compass before him. Grimwald went cringing forward, his shaking hands outstretched—

'I didn't mean to kill!' he croaked; and went stumbling to his knees. 'I swear it! Don't follow me! We were friends once—mercy, mercy!'

A shout from the captain.

'What's that ahead? Look out, man!'

'Nothing ahead, sir; fog lifting!'

'God, I almost felt it!'

The captain wiped his streaming forehead, but Grimwald neither saw nor heard. He was looking at Calderwood, a twisted grin on his face, his big hands waving persuasively.

'Get back—get back!' he stammered. 'Get your lifebelt; we're going to strike, Calderwood!' He laughed long and terribly. 'Come along; get your lifebelt,' he whispered. 'I've got mine. They'll pick us up. Don't stand there looking at me, damn you!' he snarled, and whipped out his revolver. 'I shot once; I can shoot again!'

'What's that?'

Jordan saw it first and almost shrieked the words.

'Something ahead, sir!'

The warning was a terrified roar from the look-out man.

'Port your helm! Port your helm!'

It was Calderwood who spoke, and the wheel spun under the quartermaster's hand.

'My God! Full astern!'

The engines clanged as the big liner heeled over. The clang and the shot came together.

Jordan heard the shot, but he was glaring at the hull ahead—the black, lightless hull that went sweeping past on the starboard bow, so close that one might jump aboard.

Captain Manson spun round as he saw the danger drop away into the darkness of the night.

He crossed to the prostrate figure of Grimwald.

'What's wrong?' he asked.

'I don't know, sir; someone told me to port my helm!' said the white-faced quartermaster.

Jordan joined the captain, and together they knelt by his side.

'This man is dead,' said the captain, in a hushed voice.

'Dead?'

Burton turned, too full of his business to heed the minor tragedy.

'Fog lifted, sir!'

'Dead?' Manson picked up the revolver. 'Not shot?'

Jordan was examining the dead man by the light of an electric torch.

'His face is the face of a man who has seen—' He looked seriously down at the distorted features. 'I wonder what he saw?' he said, half to himself.

The Yellow Box

When Christopher Angle went to school he was very naturally called "Angel" by his fellows. When, in after life, he established a reputation for tact, geniality, and a remarkable equability, of temper, he became "Angel, Esquire," and, as Angel Esquire, he went through the greater portion of his adventurous life, so that on the coast and in the islands and in the wild lands that lie beyond the It'uri Forest, where Mr C. Angle is unknown, the remembrance of Angel, Esquire, is kept perennially green.

In what department of the Government he was before he took up a permanent suite of rooms at New Scotland Yard it is difficult to say. All that is known is that when the "scientific expedition" of Dr Kauffhaus penetrated to the head waters of the Kasakasa River, Angel Esquire, was in the neighbourhood shooting elephants. A native messenger en route to the nearest post, carrying a newly-ratified treaty, counter-signed by the native chief, can vouch for Angel's presence, because Angel's men fell upon him and beat him, and Angel took the newly-sealed letter and calmly tore it up.

When, too, yet another "scientific expedition," was engaged in making elaborate soundings in a neutral port in the Pacific, it was his steam launch that accidentally upset the boat of the men of science, and many invaluable instruments and drawings were irretrievably lost in the deeps of the rocky inlet. Following, however, upon some outrageous international incident, no less than the—but perhaps it would be wiser not to say—Angel was transferred bodily to Scotland Yard, undisguisedly a detective, and was placed in charge of the Colonial Department, which deals with all matters in those countries — British or otherwise—where the temperature rises above 103 degrees Fahrenheit. His record in this department was one of unabated success, and the interdepartmental criticism which was aroused by its creation and his appointment, have long since been silenced by the remarkable success that attended, amongst others, his investigations into the strange disappearance of the Corringham Mine, the discovery of the Third Slave, and his brilliant and memorable work in connection with the Croupier's Safe.

To Angel, Esquire, in the early spring came an official of the Criminal Investigation Department.

"Do you know Congoland at all, Angel?" he asked.

"Little bit of it," said Angel modestly.

"Well, here's a letter that the chief wants you to deal with—the writer is the daughter of an old friend, and he would like you to give the matter your personal attention."

Angel's insulting remark about corruption in the public service need not be placed on record.

The letter was written on notepaper of unusual thinness.

"A lady who has had or is having correspondence with somebody in a part of the world where the postage rate is high," he said to himself, and the first words of the letter confirmed this view:

"My husband, who has just returned from the Congo, where he has been on behalf of a Belgian firm to report on alluvial gold discoveries, has become so strange in his manner, and there are, moreover, such curious circumstances in connection with his conduct, that I am taking this course, knowing that as a friend of my dear father's you will not place any unkind construction upon it, and that you will help me to get at the bottom of this mystery."

The letter was evidently hurriedly written. There were words crossed out and written in.

"Humph," said Angel; "rather a miserable little domestic drama. I trust I shall not be called in to investigate every family jar that occurs in the homes of the chief's friends."

But he wrote a polite little note to the lady on his "unofficial" paper, asking for an appointment and telling her that he had been asked to make the necessary enquires. The next morning he received a wire inviting him to go to Dulwich to the address that had appeared at the head of the note. Accordingly he started that afternoon, with the irritating sense that his time was being wasted.

Nine hundred and three Lordship Lane was a substantial-looking house, standing back from the road, and a trim maid opened the door to him, and ushered him into the drawing-room.

He was waiting impatiently for the lady, when the door was flung open and a man staggered in. He had an opened letter in his hand, and there was a look on his face that shocked Angel. It was the face of a soul in torment—drawn, haggard, and white.

"My God! my God!" he muttered: then he saw Angel, and straightened himself for a moment, for he started forward and seized the detective by the arm eagerly.

"You—you," he gasped, "are you from Liverpool? Have they sent you down to say it was a mistake?"

There was a rustle of a dress, and a girl came into the room. She was little more than a girl, but the traces of suffering that Angel saw had aged her. She came quickly to the side of the man and laid her hand on his arm.

"What is it—oh, what is it, Jack?" she entreated.

The man stepped back, shaking his head. "I'm sorry, ver' sorry," he said dully, and Angel noticed that he clipped his words. "I thought—I mistook this gentleman for someone else."

Angel explained his identity to the girl in a swift glance.

"This—this is a friend of mine," she faltered, "a friend of my father's," she went on hesitatingly, "who has called to see me."

"Sorry—sorry," he said stupidly. He stumbled to the door and went out, leaving it open. They heard him blundering up the stairs, and after a while a door slammed, and there came a faint "click" us he locked it.

"Oh, can you help me?" cried the girl in distress. "I am beside myself with anxiety."

"Please sit down, Mrs Farrow," said Angel hastily, but kindly. A woman on the verge of tears always alarmed him. Already he felt an unusual interest in the case. "Just tell me from the beginning."

"My husband is a metallurgist, and a year ago, he was commissioned by a Belgian company interested in gold-mining to go to the Congo and report on some property there."

"Had he ever been there before?"

"No; he had never been to Africa before. It was against my wish that he went at all, but the fee was so temptingly high, and the opportunities so great, that I yielded to his persuasion, and allowed him to go."

"How did he leave you?"

"As he had always been—bright, optimistic, and full of spirits. We were very happily married, Mr Angel—" she stopped, and her lips quivered.

"Yes, yes," said the alarmed detective; "please go on."

"He wrote by every mail, and even sent natives in their canoes hundreds of miles to connect with the mail steamers, and his letters were bright and full of particulars about the country and the people. Then, quite suddenly, they changed. From being the cheery, long letters they had been, they became almost notes, telling me just the bare facts of his movements. They worried me a little, because I thought it meant that he was ill, had fever, and did not want me to know."

"And had he?"

"No. A man who was with him said he was never once down with fever. Well, I cabled to him, but cabling to the Congo is a heart-breaking business, and there was fourteen days' delay on the wire."

"I know," said Angel sympathetically, "the land wire down to Brazzaville."

"Then, before my cable could reach him, I received a brief telegram from him saying he was coming home."

"Yes?"

"There was a weary month of waiting, and then he arrived. I went to Southampton to meet him."

"To Southampton, not to Liverpool?"

"To Southampton. He met me on the deck, and I shall never forget the look of agony in his eyes when he saw me. It struck me dumb. 'What is the matter, Jack?' I asked. 'Nothing,' he said, in, oh, such a listless, hopeless way. I could get nothing from him. Almost as soon as he got home he went to his room and locked the door."

"When was this?"

"A month ago."

"And what has happened since?"

"Nothing; except that he has got steadily more and more depressed, and—and—"

"Yes?" asked Angel.

"He gets letters—letters that he goes to the door to meet. Sometimes they make him worse, sometimes he gets almost cheerful after they arrive; but he had his worst bout after the arrival of the box."

"What box?"

"It came whilst I was dressing for dinner one night. All that afternoon he had been unusually restless, running down from his room at every ring of the bell. I caught a glance of it through his half-opened door."

"Do you not enter his room occasionally?"

She shook her head. "Nobody has been into his room since his return; he will not allow the servants in, and sweeps and tidies it himself."

"Well, and the box?"

"It was about eighteen inches high, and twelve inches square. It was of polished yellow wood."

"Did it remind you of anything?"

"Of an electric battery," she said slowly. "One of those big portable things that you can buy at an electrician's."

Angel thought deeply.

"And the letters—have you seen them?" he asked.

"Only once, when the postman overlooked a letter, and came back with it. I saw it for a moment only, because my husband came down immediately and took it from me."

"And the postmark?"

"It looked like Liverpool," she said.

He questioned her again on one or two aspects that interested him.

"I must see your husband's room," he said decisively.

She shook her head.

"I am afraid it will be impossible," she said.

"We shall see," said Angel cheerfully.

Then an unearthly chattering and screeching met their ears, and the girl turned pale.

"Oh, I had forgotten the most unpleasant thing—the monkey!" she said, and beckoned him from the room. He passed through the house to the garden at the back. Well sheltered from the road was a big iron cage, wherein sat a tiny Congo monkey, shivering in the chill spring air, and drawing about his hairy shoulders the torn half of a blanket.

"My husband brought one home with him," she said, "but it died. This is the fifth monkey we have had in a month, and he, poor beastie, does not look as if he were long for life."

The little animal fixed his bright eyes on Angel, and chattered dismally.

"They get ill, and my husband shoots them," the girl went on. "I wanted him to let a veterinary surgeon see the last one, but he would not."

"Curious," said Angel musingly, and, after making arrangements to call the next morning, he went back to his office in a puzzled frame of mind.

He duly reported to his chief the substance of his interview.

"It isn't drink, and it isn't drugs," he said. "To me it looks like sheer panic. If that man is not in mortal fear of somebody or something, I am very much mistaken."

The girl had given him some of the earlier letters she had received from Africa, and after dinner that night Angel sat down in his little flat in Jermyn Street to read them. In the first letter —it was dated Boma—occurred a passage that gave him pause. After telling how he had gone ashore at Flagstaff, and had made a little excursion up one of the rivers, the letter went on to say:

"Apparently, I have quite unwillingly given deep offence to one of the secret societies—if you can imagine a native secret society—by buying from a native a most interesting ju-ju or idol. The native, poor beggar, was found dead on the beach this morning; and although the official view is that he was bitten by a poisonous snake, I feel that his death had something to do with the selling of the idol, which, by the way, resembles nothing so much as a decrepit monkey...."

In his search through the letters he could find no other reference to the incident, except in one of the last of the longer epistles, where he found:

"... the canoe overturned, and we were struggling in the water. To my intense annoyance, amongst other personal effects lost was the coast ju-ju I wrote to you about. A missionary who lives close at hand said the current, not being strong about here, the idol is recoverable, and has promised to send a boy down first, and if he finds it to send it on to me. I have given him our address at home in case it turns up...."

"In case it turns up!" repeated Angel. "I wonder—"

He knew of these extraordinary societies. He knew, too, how strong a hold they had in the country that lay behind Flagstaff. These dreadful organisations were not to be lightly dismissed. Their power was indisputable.

"The question is, how far are they responsible for the present trouble," he said, discussing the affair with his chief the next morning, "how far the arm of the offended ju-ju can reach. If we were on the coast I should not be surprised to find our young friend dead in his bed any morning. But we are in England— and in Dulwich to boot!"

"The yellow box may explain everything," said his chief thoughtfully.

"And I mean to see it to-day," said Angel determinedly. He did not see it that day, for on his return to his office he found a telegram awaiting him from Mrs Farrow:

PLEASE COME AT ONCE. MY HUSBAND DISAPPEARED LAST NIGHT AND HAS NOT RETURNED. HE HAS TAKEN WITH HIM THE BOX AND THE MONKEY.

He was ringing at the door of the house within an hour after receiving the telegram. Her eyes were red with weeping: and it was a little time before she could speak. Then, brokenly, she told the story of her husband's disappearance. It was after the household had retired for the night she thought she heard a vehicle draw up at the door. She was half asleep, but the sound of voices roused her, and she got out of bed and looked through the Venetian blinds. Her room faced the road, and she could see a carriage drawn up opposite the gate. A man walking beside her husband, who carried a box, which she recognised as the yellow box, and in the strange man's arms she could discern, by the light of the street lamp, a quivering bundle which proved to be the monkey.

Before she could move or raise the window her husband entered the carriage, taking with him the monkey, and the other man jumped up by the side of the driver as the vehicle drove off, and, as he did, she saw his face. It was that of a negro.

Angel suppressed the exclamation that sprang to his lips as he heard this. It was evident that she had not attached any importance to the story of the ju-ju, and he did not wish to alarm her.

"Did he leave a message?"

She handed him a sheet of paper without replying. Only a few lines were scrawled on the sheet:—

"I am a moral coward, darling, and dare not tell you. If I come back, you will know why I have left you. If not, pray for me, and remember mo kindly. I have placed all my money to the credit of your hanking account."

The girl was crying quietly.

"Let me see his room," said Angel; and she conducted him to the little apartment that was half laboratory and half study. A truckle bed ran lengthways beneath, the window, and a heap of blackened ashes were piled up in the fireplace.

"Nothing has been touched," said the girl.

Gingerly, Angel lifted the curling ashes one by one.

"I've known burnt paper to..."—he was going to say "hang a man," but altered it to "be of great service."

There were one or two pieces that the fire had not burnt, and some on which the letters were still discernible. One of these he lifted and carried to the window.

"Hullo!" he muttered.

He could not find a complete sentence, but, as he read it: ... very bad ... monkey ... take you away ... your own fault....

There was a blotting pad upon the little table, and a square dust mark, where he surmised, the mysterious box stood. He lifted the pad; underneath were a number of strips of paper.

He glanced at them carelessly, then:

"What on earth?" he said.

Indelibly printed on the slips before him were a dozen red thumb prints.

He looked at them closely.

The thumb prints were of blood!

Then, in the midst of his mystification a light dawned on Angel, and he turned to the girl.

"Has you husband bought a methylated spirit lamp lately?" he asked.

She looked at him in astonishment.

"Why, yes," she said, "a fortnight ago he bought one."

"And has he been asking for needles?"

She almost gasped.

"Yes, yes, almost every day!"

Angel looked again at the charred paper and smiled.

"Of course, this may be serious," he said; "but really I think it isn't at all. If you will content your mind for a day, I will tell how serious it is; if you will extend your content for four days, I would almost undertake to promise to restore him to you."

He left her that afternoon in an agony of suspense, and three hours afterwards she received a telegram:

FOUND YOUR HUSBAND—EXPECT HIM HOME TO-MORROW.

To his chief Angel explained the mystery in three minutes.

"I thought the ju-ju had nothing to do with it," he said cheerfully. "The whole thing illustrates the folly of a man who had never been further from home than Wiesbaden penetrating God's primaeval forest. Farrow, on the Congo, surrounded on all sides by the disease, must needs be suddenly obsessed by the belief that he has sleeping-sickness. So home he comes, filled with dread forebodings, and visions of the madness that comes to the people, with trypanosomiasis. Buys microscopes—our yellow box—and jabs his finger day by day to examine his blood for microbes. As soon as I heard he had got the approved spirit lamp for sterilising purposes, I knew that. He corresponds with the Tropical Schools of Medicine in London and Liverpool, boring those poor people to death with his outrageous symptoms. Jabs his blood into monkeys, and when they die—of cold and bad feeding—fears the worst. So, at last, some wise doctor at the London School, after writing and telling him that he was an ass, that he couldn't be very bad, and that the monkey's death wasn't any sign—except of cruelty to animals —offers to take him into hospital for a few days and put him under observation. So along comes the hospital carriage, with their nigger porter, and away goes our foolish hypochondriac, with his monkey and his box of tricks. They are turning him out of hospital to-morrow."

When the Armanic Sank

" Marjorie Swain," said her uncle solemnly, "you are going to end up by marrying a tramp."

The girl, sitting on the end of the sofa swinging her foot, laughed.

Marjorie was difficult. She was very rich, and she was very pretty. She was also something of a student of affairs, wrote clever articles in The Woman's Age, and was voted eccentric by some, as unwomanly by others, and as somewhat unapproachable by most people. Only in books and stories are very pretty women, who are also very rich, surrounded by crowds of suitors. Men, on the whole, are too vain to crowd round a woman, however much in love, or in debt, they may be.

Uncle Gordon lit a fresh cigar and looked up at her quizzically.

"Marjie,"he said, "strong-minded young ladies like you end by marrying burglars."

"It must be interesting to marry a burglar—a nice, brave, Raffles person,"she meditated.

"Hmp!" growled her uncle. "The men who catch women like you aren't either nice or brave—look there!"

He pointed through the window. A disconsolate newsboy stood in the drizzling rain clutching a contents bill:

EXTRADITION
Of
DR. BALSCOMBE

She laughed long and gleefully, throwing back her head in an ecstasy of bubbling amusement.

"Oh, uncle! Am I as bad as that—am I likely to marry Dr. Balscombe?" she asked in mock concern.

"I think nobody is likely to marry the doctor," said her relative, drawing steadily at his cigar, "he'll hang—but he is an instance of the man who captivates impossible women—that is to say, impossible to any other kind of man—by sheer fascination and blarney. If he hadn't killed two poor souls for the vulgar insurance money one could have admired his gifts."

She slipped down from the end of the couch and walked to the window.

"I've read every scrap of the evidence against him," she said, "and if the case hadn't ended yesterday I should have delayed leaving for America. Lady Grancely wanted me to go to court and see him."

Gordon Brebent muttered something about "idle, morbid women," but she ignored his offensiveness. Uncle Gordon was a dear, but somewhat old-fashioned. She walked back to where he sprawled, a model of comfortable inelegance, and laid her hand on his shoulder.

"Come and see me off to-morrow, and I promise not to talk about the wicked doctor," she said.

Gordon Brebent promised and kept his word.

If the truth be told, Marjorie did not keep hers, but that was due to a locked railway compartment with drawn blinds, and the whisper that ran along the boat train that the criminal, whose name had been in everybody's mouth, was a fellow-passenger.

She learnt much from her somewhat stodgy fellows of the first saloon, and might have learnt much more but for the fact that, when the Armanic was fifty miles from Queenstown, and Marjorie was dozing in her deck chair, oblivious of the sudden excitement which thrilled the ship, something struck the great liner amidships—something that exploded with a crash like thunder and sent a white, solid column of water leaping into the air before it trembled and broke upon the dumb-stricken passengers.

An hour later she was still without any clear recollection of what had happened.

She looked back over the grey hummocks of water and could see nothing save the blur of the smoke from a disappearing drifter. Instinctively she glanced at her watch. It was three o'clock. So the watch was watertight. It was curious that she should remember the shopman's guarantee.

Three o'clock! There were five hours of light left—at least. What time did the sun set? She knitted her pretty forehead trying to remember. She usually dressed for dinner at 7.30, and it was not dark then. It was not even dark at 8.15 when she left her room. Nine o'clock—perhaps later. She raised her hand very gingerly and pushed back the long, soddened snakes of hair from her face. Even the salt water had not dimmed its bronze splendour.

She had need to move cautiously, because she was sitting astride of a small but buoyant bale, that bobbed and rose with the sea and threatened to capsize if she departed by a single inch breadth from her centre of balance.

The young man who swam by her side had all his eyes for the dim line of land to the north. He had a patent life-saving waistcoat about his body, and presented a somewhat bloated appearance.

Now and again he would lift his hand and give the little bale a push in the direction he wanted it to take, for he was rudder and motor power to the frail raft on which Marjorie Swain sat.

"It's awfully uncomfortable," she said, with a quick smile in answer to something he had said, "but it's ever so much nicer than being drowned."

She turned as she spoke and nearly overbalanced herself.

"Hold on!" he warned, and shot up his hand to steady her. "I guess you'd better take your skirt off, my friend—if it is possible."

She looked straight ahead.

"It is quite possible,"she said, "but I shall have to come into the water to do it." He held out his hand and she slipped from her perch.

He held her unceremoniously enough by the scruff of her neck, for she needed both hands.

"That's better, I think," he said, after the struggle which preceded her return to the bale.

She said nothing, not knowing exactly what a lady, clad grotesquely in a Paquin blouse and black silk knickers, should say to a very self-possessed young stranger whom she had never met before until he had grabbed her by the hair and pushed and hauled her to temporary safety.

"What was it struck us? "she asked, after a while.

"A torpedo. I saw the submarine before it struck—at least I saw the periscope."

A pause.

"Rather beastly of them, wasn't it?" She shuddered at a certain terrible memory.

"Fairly fierce," he answered nonchalantly.

Another long pause, broken only by a smothered exclamation on the part of the girl when, in heading the raft to its course, he had all but overbalanced her.

"We're in—in danger rather, aren't we? "she asked presently.

He looked up and his eyes met hers. She realised, with a little sense of amused surprise, that she had not looked at him before. He was good-looking and something more. There was a certain hardy healthiness in his face, which told of a life spent mainly in the open.

"It all depends,"he answered cautiously. "That streak of grey is Ireland, and round about here we ought to strike a fishing-boat or two. Had you anybody with you on board?"

She shook her head and sighed.

"That's a relief," he said cheerfully. "Well, I could echo that sigh."

He swam lazily, using only one hand, and she wondered why. She thought of asking him when he spoke.

"Was there anybody on board you knew?" he asked.

She shook her head again.

"With one exception they were the most uninteresting crowd of people I ever met," she said. "Had you anybody with you?" He nodded.

"Somebody—somebody you were attached to?" she asked, and there was a pleasant little thrill of anxiety in her voice.

"Yes," he said, and she thought his tone sounded a little unsympathetic. But men hide their grief that way, she remembered.

"You were saying there was an exception in that commonplace crowd?" he said.

She looked down at him.

"I should have imagined that you knew," she said, "everybody on board knew—it was in the newspapers."

"I never read the newspapers," he said; "you see—steady!"

She was swaying wildly, and he put out his right hand to steady her. It was strange that he always gave her the hand he swam with. Perhaps he had injured the other.

"Tell me about your interesting man who was in all the newspapers," he said, after she had again recovered her sense of equation. "I am very keen on interesting men."

"Dr. Balscombe," she said briefly. "Of course he is a horrible person—but women are interested in those kind of people, even nice women. I suppose it is the working of their insatiable curiosity. Just as they want to see what is the best in man, so they want to glimpse something of the worst. People call it morbidity, but in reality it is the anxiety of every person present to learn what he or she has escaped."

"You're American, aren't you?" he asked, and she smiled.

"Boston," she answered demurely.

"That's near enough. I'm—I'm—well, I don't exactly know what I am. My father was Irish, my mother was a Scot, and I was born in Gibraltar."

"What do you call yourself?"

"Canadian," he replied, with charming inconsequence. "You see I've lived there for quite a long time. Well, did you see Dr. Balscombe?"

He asked this keeping his eyes on hers, and swimming easily on his side.

"No—I'm rather glad I didn't. They kept him hidden away somewhere. You know—but, of course, you don't know, if you do not read the papers—he is a very dangerous character. I think if I were a man who had murdered two wives I should be a dangerous character, too. They kept him handcuffed—the steward told me—and were so anxious to get him back to Canada for trial that the Canadian Government sent over a special police official to watch him."

"The devil they did!" said the stranger.

The land was perceptibly nearer. The girl, balanced on the bale, could distinguish the white specks of cottages near the thread width of beach.

"It is a long way yet," said the man, as if reading her thoughts, "but there will be a whole fleet of fishing-boats out, as soon as the news of the ship's foundering is telegraphed along the coast."

She strained her eyes toward the shore, and for the first time the full realisation of her danger came to her and her lips quivered.

"Now then!" he said sharply. "Go on talking—tell me something more about your Dr. Balscombe."

She shuddered.

"Please, I don't want to talk any more—are you sure that we aren't drifting?"

"Go on talking," he repeated imperiously. "You're on the verge of a breakdown, my friend."

"I'm not!" she denied indignantly. "But I'm cold, and hungry, and miserable. I don't want to talk about a brute who killed women for the sheer joy of killing them."

"And you have a little lump at the back of your throat which you're trying to swallow—it is called the bolus hystericus, and it can't be swallowed."

"Are you a doctor? "she asked.

He hesitated.

"I'm a sort of a doctor," he confessed, "but don't rely upon me to be of any assistance to you in the event of your getting panicky."

She turned sharply with a scornful retort and nearly overbalanced. So nearly, that he was surprised, not only into raising his inevitable right hand to save her, but into lifting himself so that, beneath the surface of the water, his left hand was visible also. She looked and saw, and, for a moment, she thought she would swoon.

For about his left hand, unmistakable even in the brief glimpse she secured, was the bright steel clamp of a handcuff!

She recovered her balance and her self-command at one and the same time.

For the first time that day she was frightened. The sinking of the Armanic was little more than an exciting adventure compared with this greater and more terrible experience.

"I think there is a boat coming our way," the man said suddenly. "Have you anything you could wave to attract its attention?"

She had a handkerchief, but it was no more than a sodden little ball. She took it from her belt and regarded it ruefully.

"Squeeze it out and hold it up—it will be quite dry before the boat comes anywhere near."

There was a long and strained silence.

The girl was thinking rapidly. For the first time she realised that she owed this man something—perhaps her life. She had not even a dim idea as to what had happened between the crash of the explosion, which had awakened her, and the finding of herself perched upon the little bale. Yet she must have enjoyed a lucid period, for it was quite impossible to have gained her position without some effort on her own part.

She must know before she could balance accounts between herself and him.

"Will you tell me how I was rescued?" she asked sharply.

He did not reply at first.

"I think you rescued yourself," he answered, after the pause. "At least," he corrected, "with very little assistance from me."

"How did I find this?" she asked, nodding down at her support.

"That was my bale," he confessed, "but quite unnecessary, as I had a life- saving waistcoat—so I just helped you on to it. And we sort of drifted away from the boats and here we are!"

So she did owe him her life!

She was confronted with the most painful dilemma that could face any human being. She was moving toward safety, thanks to the heroism of a convicted murderer—a man whose crimes had sent a thrill of horror through the civilised world. There was no question of Dr. Balscombe's guilt. She had read every scrap of the evidence, and knew there was no loophole of escape left to him.

That brown sail, now making directly for them, meant life and comfort for her—for the man it meant an ignominious death. She set her teeth and faced the naked verities of the situation. This man's life was forfeit to the State.

"What will you do when you get on board?" she demanded.

"Borrow a dry suit," he answered cheerfully.

"And after—when you get to land—and the police--"

She had to make a supreme effort to get the word out.

"The police?" he asked. "I see—you know?"

She nodded, still keeping her gaze directed from the upturned face.

Otherwise she might have seen evidence of his exhaustion, the hollowness of his eyes, the blue lips and pinched cheek.

"I shall just report—but don't make me talk, please."

His voice had dropped to a whisper.

She looked at him in alarm. He had stopped swimming, and his head was sinking forward till it almost touched the water.

To slip from the bale was the work of a second. With her right arm hugging the precious float, she raised his head with her disengaged hand.

It fell back wearily against her shoulder. She looked wildly, around.

"Thank God!" she said.

The boat with the brown sail was bearing down upon them. She had a half- formed plan in her mind and now it took shape.

She let go his head, lifted the manacled hand to the water's level, and endeavoured so to wrap her handkerchief about it that the handcuff was hidden. But it was too bulky. Perhaps he had a handkerchief. She searched the nearest pocket and discovered a big water-soaked bandana.

As best she could with one hand she muffled the offending wrist.

"Don't touch this bandage..." was the last thing she said to the bald-headed Irish fisherman, who hauled them to the untidy deck of his smack, before she, too, collapsed.

Two hours later they were sitting one on either side of a big, smoky, peat fire in a low-roofed cottage. He was his normal self, which meant that he was flippant and extremely amusing—or he would have been but for the trouble that was at the back of the girl's mind.

He had, she noticed, rid himself in some way of the handcuff, which was a relief.

She had had the greater part of an hour to formulate her plan for loosing on to the world the most cold-blooded scoundrel in the annals of criminality, but she did not know how to commence.

"I suppose you know," she began awkwardly, "that I am very well off."

"Yes," he said, "I am very sorry."

"Sorry!"

He nodded.

"Sorry," he repeated. "It robs the adventure of half the romance—now if you had been poor, or just comfortably well-to-do, instead of being Marjorie Swain, a dollar millionaire--"

"How did you know my name?" she asked.

He laughed.

"Just now you were taking it for granted that I knew everything about you," he mocked. "The kindly handkerchief you used--"

She went very red. She had forgotten her handkerchief on his wrist under his own.

"It was fortunate that you had your full name embroidered," he went on, "but, as I was saying, if you hadn't been rich, I should imagine myself to be in love with you."

She rose to her feet.

"How dare you!" she gasped. "You! You!--"

And yet—such was the extraordinary fascination of this man, she felt something of happiness in his calm declaration. She herself realised this and went on hastily, almost incoherently:

"I was going to say—I am well off and I am under an obligation to you. I am going to do a wicked thing—get you away from here. I have twenty pounds—it was in my belt pocket—go to London and see me there. I will give you a thousand pounds to--"

The door opened behind her and the mellow voice of the fisherman tenant announced:

"It's the police, yer honours."

She sat up rigidly and looked at the man with terror in her eyes.

Again she experienced that strange thrill, sympathy—pity—liking.

As for the man, he smiled at the big red-faced inspector of Irish Constabulary, who had followed the fisherman into the room. "You got my message?"

"Yes, sir."

"Did you find him?"

"Yes, sir," said the inspector, "one of the boats picked him up—dead."

The man nodded gravely.

"I gave him a chance for his life—I had just time to unlock the handcuff that bound us together before I was thrown into the water. I had to keep close to him until we were clear of the coast."

The girl stared at him.

"Who are you?" she asked in a whisper; "I am Dr. Mallington of the Canadian Prison Service," he said, "and, until recently, attached—I think you say attached?—to the late Dr. Balscombe."

He waited until the inspector had left the room and then leant forward.

"We were interrupted at a very exciting part of your proposal," he said, and had the audacity to take one of her hands. "What happens after you give me all this money—do I furnish a home or something?"

She laughed a little shakily, but she did not withdraw her hand.

The Devil Light

I

Some men have an aversion to cats, others shrink back in horror from a third floor window and fight desperately to overcome the temptation to throw themselves into the street below. For others the mirror holds a devil who leers a man on to self-destruction. But for Hans Richter that cruel and puzzling light which he interpreted into E Flat held all that there was of threat and fear.

If you say that the obsession of little Hans savoured of madness, tell me something of yourself. Squeak a knife-edge along a plate, or knife-edge against knife-edge and watch the people shudder and grimace. They also are mad of the same madness. Some men and women grow frantic at the rustle of silk; others may not pass their palms over certain surfaces (such as plush or velvet) without a shivering fit. Exactly why, nobody knows.

There are undreamt of horrors in commonplace objects for some of us—Hans Richter had the advantage of hating and fearing that which was not commonplace.

He played second violin at the Hippoleum. He had little spare time with a daily matinée and a twelve o'clock rehearsal every Monday, but he utilized that spare time with great profit, being a most earnest student of colour values, and, moreover, a worshipper of heroes.

You had no doubt as to what manner of heroes qualified for his adoration. Nature had built him short and clumsy, with a pink, round face and blue eyes. She had built him cheap as a builder runs up a cottage out of the material left over from a more pretentious job.

'Well buttressed, but poorly thatched,' he described himself, and indeed the great Dame had been mean in the matter of head-covering, for his hair, sandy and fine, was in a quantity less than was necessary. His moustaches were mere wisps, but in the shape to which he trained them you read his mind, his faith and his pride.

He was a gentle soul, with strange and unusual views on lights, and a certain pride in his intimate knowledge of London. It was his boast that there was not a street in the metropolitan area which he had not visited, not a historic monument upon which he could not enlarge at length; and once on a more than ordinarily poisonous night of fog he had led Sam Burns by the hand from Holborn Town-Hall to Paddington Station, and never bungled a single crossing, never so much as mistook the entrance of a blind alley, though the fog was so thick that Sam could neither see his guide nor the pavement under his feet.

Oh, no, he was no spy—he hated the Prussian, as so many Bavarians did before the war (he was from Nurnberg). He was German all through, but neither favoured bureaucracy nor militarism.

They lived together, this curious pair, in a tiny house off Church Street, Paddington—in a neighbourhood of strange smells and of Sunday morning markets. Sam Burns was 'Mr Burns' in law, and entitled (did they but know it) to the respectful salute of policemen, for he was a naval gunner on the reserve of officers, and held the King's warrant.

They had one quality in common—that they were simple men — and because of this No 43 Bebchurch Street was a haven of peace.

For Sam directed such casual help as he could secure in his best quarter-deck manner, had a gift for spying out untidy corners and hurried scrubbings, a vigilance which earned for him the hatred and slander of the charladies of Paddington, and resulted in a constant melancholy procession of new servants.

They sat together by an open window on a Sunday evening in June 1914, taking the air. Sam's lean red face was one great scowl, for he was reading a thrilling murder case—facial contortion was part of the process of his reading.

'Murder's a curious thing,' he said at last, setting the paper down on his knee. 'I've killed men in my time—natives and that sort of thing—but always in what I might term the heat of battle. I wonder how it feels?'

Hans turned his mild face to the other and stared through his gold-rimmed glasses.

'Herr Gott!' he said. 'That you should talk about such subjects, Sam—who could think of murder on such a night? It is a night for thought—exalted thought!'

He stopped suddenly, pursing his lips and looking thoughtfully out of the open window, and upward to the patch of western sky which showed above the mean housetops.

'G minor,' he said abstractedly, and Sam grinned.

'You're mad on lights, Hans!" he chuckled. 'G minor!—what the dickens is G minor?'

Without turning his head or relinquishing his gaze the musician whistled a soft sweet note sustained, and full of sorrow.

Sam frowned.

'I'm beginning to see,' he admitted, 'yes—that's the kind of light it is. You're a crank on lights, Hans—'

The other swung round in his chair and reached for his violin and bow that lay on the table near him. He drew the bow across the muted strings and a gloomy stream of thick sound filled the little room.

'Purple,' he said, and played another long note—a joyous blatant note of arrogant triumph.

'Scarlet,' he smiled, and put the instrument back.

'Lights are horrible or beautiful—terrifying or adorable — listen.'

He seized the instrument again and sent the bow rasping across the strings.

'For God's sake don't make that infernal noise!' growled Sam shifting uneasily, for the note shrill and menacing carried terror in its volume.

Hans had the instrument on his knees. His lids were narrowed, his plump jaw outthrust.

'That is white light—the devil's light—cruel and searching. It stares and shrieks at me. There is a beckoning devil in that light. You see it on the stage—I have seen it a hundred times. It strips young girls of their modesty, it reveals the lie, it mocks the passé. You can see them staring at it—blinded and yet staring, their white teeth glittering, their red lips smiling like children smile when they are in pain—it is the light of war, and cruelty and suffering—phew!'

He flung the violin away and mopped his damp forehead with a big green handkerchief.

Sam rose from his window chair slowly.

'Hans, you're a fool,' he said, 'and I'm going to put a B major match to the A flat lamp.'

Hans laughed and rose too with the remark:

'And I'm going to a ten o'clock rehearsal—the show opens to- morrow—Gott! It is a quarter to ten already!'

It was not a happy rehearsal for the little German. There was a new American producer at the Hippoleum, a burly man in a grey sweater, who was quick to wrath, and had a wealth of unpleasant language.

In the third scene the lights went wrong. Four specially erected electric projectors had been fixed in the gallery, and on a certain chord, at the end of a song number, they had to concentrate upon the principal, who was singing. And they just didn't. One wandered off to the second entrance. One wavered undecidedly too far up stage, and the other two did not appear at all.

'Say, what's the matter with you?' exploded the producer. 'Are you crazy up there? Is this a joke?'

He said other sarcastic things, and said them through a megaphone, which somehow made them worse.

A hollow and apologetic voice answered from the deserted gallery.

'Put all your lines down—now put 'em on the proscenium arch—now put 'em all together up stage—now put 'em on the bald-headed fiddler in the orchestra—'

There was a gentle titter of laughter from the weary chorus—but it was short-lived.

The bald-headed fiddler was standing up facing the light, his face distorted with rage, his wild eyes glaring like a trapped animal, as his clawing hands flung out at the light.

A torrent of words, German and English, poured from his twisted mouth.

'Take it off! Take it off! Take it off!' he screamed.

There was an instant and a painful pause. The lights dimmed and an outraged producer strode down the central aisle of the theatre and confronted the second violin.

'For the lord's sake!' he said, mildly enough, 'have you gone mad, mister?'

The little man, one trembling hand curved about the orchestra rail, shook his head. He was very white, and the American, a judge of men, and kindly enough out of business hours, dropped his big hand on the other's shoulder.

'You go right along home and have a sleep, son,' he said gently; 'don't you worry—go right along home.'

'It's the light, sir,' faltered Hans, and blinked fearfully up at the gallery. I do not like the light—'

'Sure!' soothed the other; 'now you go right away and have a rest — there's nothin' comin' to you, son—on the square. I get just crazy like that myself.'

Hans did not lose his job—he played second fiddle on the opening night of that brilliant success, There You Are, Bunny!and would have gone on playing through the inevitable run but for certain great happenings in Europe. A prince of an Imperial house was killed, and when the message came to six chancelleries six separate and distinct ministers demanded of their war offices, 'How soon can you mobilize?'

Hans did not know this, but later he was to have misgivings.

'I must go home,' he said doggedly. 'I am too old to be of any use — but who knows?'

He looked wistfully at the red-faced Mr Burns, who sprawled across the table gloating over a newspaper chart which showed the relative proportions of the world's fleets.

Sam looked up.

'They'll want me,' he said with quiet satisfaction. 'My old captain will hoist his flag—he's vice admiral now—and he promised me that if ever there was a kick-up he'd take me. Who made the Penelope the best gunnery ship in the home fleet? Me, Hans!'

He thumped his thick chest and his eyes were puckered with proud laughter.

'I'm not too old for sea-going, but if I am there are lots of jobs for a man who ain't too old to spot a damned—'

He stopped in confusion. The eyes of Hans were set and the dominant expression in those eyes was envy.

'Gott!' he said with a sigh, 'I am no good—I hate war — it is terrible to think about—it is like the white light, a devil! But I must go back. Perhaps I may take the place of one—if He wants me!'

He left the next day—an exhilarating day for Mr Burns, for he had received a notification that 'my lords of the Admiralty' had accepted his offer of service.

Hans, with his brown ulster and his aged violin, came, packed his cheap gripsack and two brown paper parcels, paid his share of the expenses which were current, and went off in a taxicab.

'Good-by, Sam.'

'Good-by, Hans—good luck!'

The little man's grief was undisguised.

'I shall think of you—as a soft golden light, Sam,' he choked.

'That's right,' replied his less imaginative friend, 'yellow for me, Hans.'

Poor old Hans! So thought Mr Gunner Burns with a sigh...anyway, they weren't likely to meet. The little musician would scarcely be found amongst the ships' companies which the marksmanship of Gunner Burns foredoomed to destruction.

So passed Hans, and as for Sam, after a spell at Whale Island teaching the young and impetuous naval marksman how to shoot, he came back to Somewhere in England to more important duties.

II

There was a noise like the roll of a trap drum—an even 'br-r-r-r' of sound.

Gunner Burns standing in the darkness, dropped his head sideways and listened.

It was faint at first, but grew louder with every second that passed, and the noise came from the air.

Sam peered over the parapet in a swift, keen scrutiny of the sector south of the position. Somewhere beyond the inky belt of darkness which blotted out the nearest features of the landscape was London—London the vast and wealthy, a gigantic, flat hive buzzing and droning, unconscious of the danger.

As the watcher looked he pressed the electric button which was fixed to the wall near his hand, and almost instantly a second figure joined him.

The trap drum noise was now loud and angry, and the men craned their necks and searched the skies through their night glasses.

'There she is, sir!' said Sam in a low voice, 'the biggest they've got ... '

The officer at his side had his glasses on the lean shape that blotted no more than two or three stars at a time.

'What's her range?' he asked with the regret in his voice of one who anticipates an answer which will dash his hopes.

'Three or four thousand yards—shall I light her up?'

The other's hands had closed on the telephone receiver in the little recess beneath the parapet.

' 'Lo—that you, Shepherds Bush? Zep coming over, I'm going to light her up—no, only one as far as I can see. She'll start circling in a minute, looking for the small-arms factory as usual...Right!'

He turned to the man at his side with a grunted order. Something hissed and spluttered. Little bubbles of light outlined a big barrel shape somewhere in the rear of where he stood, and there leaped into the air a solid white beam of dazzling light which moved restlessly from side to side till it settled on something which looked for all the world like a silver cigar.

'She's just beyond range—but give her one for herself, Burns,' said the young officer. 'She's turning!'

The deafening crash of a gun woke the still night—a drift of smoke passed between the observer and his objective. As it cleared a tiny point of vivid light flicked and faded beneath the big silver cigar.

'Five hundred yards short,' was the bitter comment.

'She'll take some hitting! Keep the light on her—Shepherds Bush will pick her up in a minute...'

WHOOM!

The shock and pulsation of the explosion came to them. The trees rustled as though they had been stirred by a gust of wind, and the concrete parapet under the officer's hands trembled and shook again.

The old gunner at his side drew a sharp breath.

'Addlestone—that is!' he said. 'Fancy Addlestone! Good God, it doesn't seem real, does it? Why, when I was a kid I went to school at Addlestone...'

Another report followed, fainter than the first, and then over toward Addlestone came a red glow in the sky, a glow which gathered in brightness until it was almost golden.

'Them thermite bombs are pretty useful,' said the gunner with reluctant admiration. 'Hot! You can't get near a fire that's been started by one of them. I've seen men and women roasted to death by 'em, and they never knew what killed 'em. There's Shepherds Bush, sir!'

From the south two white beams had shot into the air and focused instantly on the fast moving cigar. She turned to the westward, and the lights followed. She moved in one majestic sweep to the east—but the lights did not leave her. They were the two great eyes of the dark world staring their wrath at the night bird.

'She wants that cloud dam' badly,' said the young naval officer. 'Put your light over the cloud—yes, it's big enough.'

He took up the telephone.

' 'Lo, Shepherds Bush...She's going for the cloud on the left. She's about level—no, I can't keep her lit up for much longer—she's getting beyond my range.'

The sky shape was now blurred and indistinct, for it had reached the misty edges of the cloud—in ten seconds it had disappeared. But now flashed into the air not two but a dozen searching eyes. They grew from the dark void beyond the hillcrest to the south, slender white spokes of light that criss-crossed incessantly. The cloud glowed yellow where the beam came to a dead end, and once it sparkled at a dozen points, For all the world, as Gunner Burns said, as if some one were striking a match along its under surface and had done no more than raise a shower of sparks.

'Shrapnel,' said the old authority approvingly; 'that'll rattle her a bit. Nothing like a nearby shell burst to make you take your eyes from the compass—there she is!'

Out she came from the same cloud-wall into which she had dived — into the gleam and glare of the searchlights. Left and right, beneath and at the side of her the light splashes came and went. They were as soft and as sudden as the glow the fireflies make.

The great machine turned again, her nose rose slowly into the air and her tail went down. The watchers could see the cloud of oily smoke at the stern as her speed increased.

'She's got to climb for it, and climb quick,' said the gunner.

A quick fan of light leapt up from the ground over by Golders Green.

WHOOM!

'A keepsake,' said the lieutenant grimly.

The telephone bell tinkled and an urgent voice demanded his immediate attention.

'She's going back to you, Carter—keep your light on her. She's twelve thousand seven hundred feet up and rising—shoot her off or she'll give you hell!'

'Ay, ay, sir!' the officer swung round. 'Light her up!'

Again the searchlight stabbed the dark, and again the cigar floated in a halo of soft radiance.

Then from the north came a new sound. It was not the 'br-r-r-r' they had heard before, but a purring note—a far-off motorcycle could reproduce the gentle din.

High above, the merest midgets in the vast space of starlit sky, three specks of earth-dust moved slowly across the field of the watchers' vision, and as they moved, in the limitless dome of the heavens a red ball of light lived and died. The young officer sought the telephone.

'Three aeroplanes up—they have signalled "shut down searchlights,"' he called breathlessly.

Two seconds passed, and then, as though one hand controlled the light shafts that swept the skies, they vanished.

They waited in the dark. The never-ceasing roar of the Zeppelin engines neither increased nor grew fainter. She was cruising laterally for some reason—the Golders Green telephone explained.

'We've hit her, sir—first or second compartment. Think one of her fore tractor screws is out of action...Yes, she got near us, but now she's drifting your way.'

'Her fourth visit,' said Sam.

'And every time she's gone straight to the place she wanted to reach,' added the officer with an impatient and wondering little 'ch'k' of his tongue. 'That fellow must know London like a book—he must know it blind to pick out his target with all the lights shaded and faked.'

Sam nodded and thought of a certain Hans Richter.

Poor old Hans! Fancy making Hans the focus of ten three-thousand candle-power searchlights! Sam grinned in the darkness.

Three...four...five minutes passed, then from the sky shot a thin beam of light that seemed from the viewpoint of the gun position to be aimed horizontally from the airship.

'Got her blinders on,' commented Sam. 'Aeroplanes are up to her level—there they are! Right ahead of her! They can do nothing with the light in their faces. She'll climb if she ain't climbing already.'

Another minute passed. Then a speck of red fire appeared in the black heavens, another red followed and then a green.

'Aeroplanes coming down—she's blinded 'em,' he said rapidly. 'Stand by to light her up—keep 'em off the aeroplanes...Now!'

From every point of the horizon the beams sprang until the sky was a thick jungle of converging light stalks. They beat fiercely, remorselessly, upon the big cigar as she zigzagged her way to safety and the north-west.

A thousand feet above the guns the landing lights of an aeroplane burnt blue, and the great bird swooped to earth. They ran out to him as the guns of Golders Green began a frantic bombardment of the disappearing Zeppelin.

It was Burns who helped the pilot to alight, and the boy who jumped to the ground was shaking from head to foot.

'Did you see it...did you see it?' he croaked. 'It was awful!'

They got him to the shelter of the position and to the little room behind. The airman was pinched and blue of face, but it was not his cold ride which had set him a tremble. He drank the cup of hot coffee they gave him, and as he did so his teeth were chattering against the edge of the mug.

'Awful!' he said at last; 'did you see it?'

'The Zep?'

He shook his head impatiently.

'No—after we gave the signal for the light, and they all came up—we were under the angle, and I looked up and suddenly a man—' he shivered and closed his eyes, 'a man leaped and straight out of the fore cabin...leaped and turned over and over...'

In the morning they made a search and found, in the big Mill Pond by Addlestone one who had in his lifetime been Hans Richter — the man who knew London and hated lights. Especially lights that could be translated into E flat.

Lord Exenham Creates a Sensation

The bombshell which Lord Exenham threw into the realms of criminal investigation will hardly be forgotten by this present generation.

It is no secret that the spring of 1914 brought a crisis in police affairs all over the world. From Yarra-Yarra to Aberdeen, from Scotland Yard to Hong Kong, police chiefs sat back and gasped, seeing the end of the most elaborate and perhaps the safest system that had ever been devised by the ingenuity of honest men for the detection of the professional criminal. For days the cables were hot with messages, and Scotland Yard, which had the matter in hand, was simply overwhelmed by the extra and unexpected work which Lord Exenham's amazing discovery necessarily involved.

MacDermot of the Central Office, New York, Pflanzer of Chicago, Maurice de Fauberg of the Sûreté were amongst those who sent special commissions to inquire into, and report upon, a happening which was very rightly regarded as revolutionising the whole system of criminal detection.

The circumstances are as follows, and they are recorded with scrupulous accuracy and impartiality in the Government report (No. 794 [Secret and Confidential] Dactylographic Committee Report), from whence the writer, who has been privileged to read the 480 pages of that report, has taken the material for this account.

On the 7th January, 1914, the Halifax premises of the British Weavers' Bank were entered by an expert bunch of 'bank-smashers', presumably an American gang which was known at the time and particulars of which had been sent forward from New York by Captain MacDermot of that city.

The burglary had been effected on the Thursday night, when it was known that large sums of money had been accumulated at the bank for the purpose of honouring the wage cheques which would be presented on the Friday morning by the various large employers of labour who used this branch.

The sum in question, some £60,000, had been brought from Leeds with an armed escort and had been safely deposited in the strong-room of the bank. As was usual on these occasions a night watchman was on duty. It was part of that duty to communicate by telephone every half-hour with the local police station.

On the night in question the calls came through regularly, and were recorded by the station sergeant. The watchman, a man named Timmers, had a very bad cold and his voice was husky, and this probably was one of the reasons contributing to the success of the burglars' coup.

At any rate the message 'All's well' reached the police station at regular intervals throughout the night until 4.30.

At 4.35, not having been signalled, the station sergeant called up the bank and received no reply. He waited a little while and again rang through, but without any greater success. Whereupon, he dispatched a sergeant and a constable to the bank, in accordance with the instructions on which this system of vigilance was conducted.

There was nothing to excite the suspicion of the patrol beyond the fact that when they knocked at the side door of the bank premises, which were in a narrow court, they received no reply.

It had been raining in the night and the constable who patrolled this beat said he himself had been several times into the court to take shelter from the exceptionally heavy downpour and that he had not noticed anything unusual. Repeated knocking having failed to elicit any answer, the manager of the bank was communicated with and drove down in his car, arriving at about 5.15.

He opened the door with his keys and the sergeant and the constable, who by this time had been joined by the inspector on duty, passed into the premises. There was no sign of disorder. A glimmering gas light still burnt and the party descended to the vaults. It was here that the worst anticipations were realised. The night watchman was discovered scientifically bound and gagged. Over his head had been drawn a canvas money bag, such as was employed by the bank for the storage of copper coinage. The door of the strong room was found open and the boxes containing the gold were missing.

The watchman was released and placed under observation, and the Halifax police immediately wired to Scotland Yard for assistance, Superintendent Branbury, of the Criminal Investigation department, arriving by the afternoon train.

The thieves had evidently effected their entrance into the premises by skeleton keys and the lock of the strong room door had been blown out by nitroglycerine. The information that the night porter could supply was not very helpful. He had been down into the vaults to make an inspection, and on returning was walking across the floor of the 'shop' when he was struck down from behind, the thieves apparently having been in the business premises of the bank for some time. He recovered consciousness to hear a hoarse voice at the telephone giving the 'All's well'. Beyond that he knew nothing.

There was only one clue discoverable in the vault, but that was an important one.

In this room was a weighing machine, and one member of the gang had with singular carelessness grasped the bright steel balance and left a perfect impression of a thumb. It was Superintendent Branbury who made this discovery, and he was destined to make another.

An engine-man on the night shift of the Halifax Milling Company had been taken ill and had been sent home by his foreman. He was still wearing the canvas-soled shoes which it was his habit to wear in the engine-room and these, in his pain, he had forgotten to change. This probably accounts for the fact that he was not heard or challenged by the robbers.

He was passing the bank on the opposite side of the road (the hour being 2.45 a.m.) when he saw three people emerge from the court and one of them, he said, was a woman.

Soon after they came into the street a big closed motor-car ran up silently and the three people returned to the court. He had a good view of only one of the men, whom he described as tall, with a 'wasp waist'. He was evidently wearing a long overcoat tightly buttoned to his figure. In the few seconds which elapsed before the arrival of the motor-car he heard the girl say, 'I am sick of it, sick of it,' and the 'wasp-waisted' man raised his hand with an extravagant gesture of menace and spoke in a high shrill voice. He did not notice or hear anything more and forgot the incident until the news of the robbery reminded him.

The motor-car was also reported as having been seen by two constables, but neither of them had taken its number.

Branbury acted quickly. The three men, the woman, and the motor-car identified the gang. It was the same confederation about whom he had been warned by the New York police and he had had at least one of them under observation.

On the following morning he journeyed to Liverpool and, accompanied by an inspector of the local police force, he went to the Callipers Hotel in Union Square. It was one of those small clean hotels, eminently sedate and respectable, with a reputation amongst commercial travellers for civility and good food, and the arrival of the police created something like a sensation.

'Yes,' said the landlord, 'there is a lady staying here, a Mrs Golding.'

Branbury nodded.

'That is the lady I want. Was she here on Thursday night?' he asked.

The landlord thought for a moment.

'I was in Manchester on Thursday night,' he said, 'but I will find out.'

His inquiries were not satisfactory. Nobody had noticed whether Mrs Golding was in or out over-night. She was certainly in the hotel on Friday, for she had slept very late.

The landlord led the way to a private sitting-room and Branbury entered unannounced.

The girl was sitting by the fire and rose to meet him. She was pretty, with a mop of golden hair and big, wistful eyes that met the detective's squarely.

'I am Superintendent Branbury, of the Criminal Investigation Department,' said Branbury, 'and I must ask you to accompany me to the police station.'

Her lids dropped and a faint smile played upon her face.

'Why, I think you have made a mistake, Mr Branbury,' she said. 'Why should I go with you to the police station?'

She was in no wise confused or agitated by a request which would have startled most people.

'I want to question you as to what you were doing on Thursday night,' said the superintendent calmly, 'and I shall also want your finger-prints.'

'Oh,' she smiled again, 'the Halifax robbery!'

'You know about that, do you?' said the detective sharply.

'Why, of course,' she drawled, 'everybody who reads the papers knows about that, Mr Branbury. If you will wait a moment I will put on my hat.'

She made a move to the other room, but Branbury followed on her heels.

'Surely you can trust me?' she asked in well-simulated surprise.

'Your name,' he said, 'is Mabel Blixon, or Jones, or Gatterley, and you are known in the United States as "California May". You are a member of a gang of bank-smashers and you have been convicted on two charges, including the shooting of a detective, for which, by a technical flaw in the evidence, you escaped punishment, and I may be excused, therefore, the indelicacy of following you to your room.'

'You have more reason to apologise for your prolixity,' she said with calm insolence.

She was searched at the police station without any discovery being made and submitted without resistance to her finger-prints being taken. From the moment Branbury compared the photograph of the impression he had taken from the scale with that of the girl's thumb-print, he was perfectly sure of his ground.

'That will do,' he said. 'I shall charge you with being concerned with three other persons in breaking and entering the premises of the British Weavers Bank at 943, High Street, Halifax.'

'Thank you very much,' she said politely.

'You have still a chance, my friend,' said the detective. He spoke from the open door of the cell into which the girl had strolled.

'Of course I have,' she said; 'by telling you my companions in crime and where the gold is hidden. Unfortunately, I am not concerned in the robbery, and though I admit that I am the lady whose history you sketched so fully, I am living a perfectly honest life and have not been concerned in any robbery in England.'

And this is the view she maintained.

She came before the stipendiary magistrate and was remanded.

A week later, on the evidence, flimsy as it was, which Branbury had collected, she was committed to take her trial at York Assizes. Branbury came back to London and interviewed the Assistant Commissioner.

'The evidence is slight,' said that individual, shaking his head, 'and I do not know that there has ever been a case where a prisoner has been convicted on finger-print evidence alone. Even in the case of the Deptford murderers there was corroborative evidence of the men having been recognised near the scene of the crime, half an hour after it had occurred.' 'Finger-print evidence is sufficient,' said Branbury; 'there is no doubt about the matter.'

'The engine-man, does he recognise her?'

Branbury shook his head.

'He failed entirely to identify the lady. I shall have to make the case as strong as possible, and I propose with your permission, sir, to call the greatest authority in London on Dactylography.'

The Commissioner raised his eyebrows.

'It is curious you should say that. I suppose you are referring to Lord Exenham?'

'Yes, sir,' nodded the detective; 'but why is that curious?'

The Commissioner pulled open a drawer and took out a letter.

'I had this from Lord Exenham this morning,' he said.

He passed the letter across to the detective, who read:

Dear Commissioner,

I am rather attracted by the Halifax Bank robbery and the interesting criminal who is charged. I hope you will give me an opportunity of making some head measurements.

Yours sincerely, EXENHAM

'I will go down and see him,' said Branbury. 'I do not think there is any chance of our lady escaping if we put Exenham in the box.'

'He will hate going into the box,' said the Commissioner, shaking his head, 'but you can try him.'

Lord Exenham, who had many claims to fame, had inherited his father's passion for data, which he had applied very largely to the study of Criminology. He had been chairman of four Commissions dealing with criminals, and had been one of the strongest supporters of the movement to introduce the finger-print system to Scotland Yard. He himself had collected, it is said, some eighty thousand impressions, and after the death of his only son and the marriage of his daughter he had practically converted Exenham Towers into a great anthropological museum.

'I have had a telegram from the Commissioner,' he said as he ushered the detective into his library, 'and I am very glad to see you, superintendent. I hope you will stay over-night.'

'I am afraid I've got to get back, sir,' said the officer.

'I am interested in this case,' Lord Exenham went on; 'but then, as you know, I am interested in all varieties of crimes and criminals.'

He looked at his big library table littered with paper and smiled.

'I am just finishing the third volume of my work on Criminal Anthropology,' he said, 'and this case rather fits an illustration of mine. Now will you please tell me the whole story?'

Briefly the detective related the story of the crime.

'It is extraordinary that the woman, who is quite young, should be so callous. I should not think she is more than twenty-six,' he said.

'I saw her photograph in the illustrated papers,' said Lord Exenham; 'in fact, it was that photograph which aroused my interest in the case. The "wasp-waisted" man—you have not found him?'

'No, my lord,' said the other; 'we have searched everywhere and the woman will tell us nothing.'

'It is very curious, very curious,' said Lord Exenham, drumming his fingers on the table. 'I suppose that girl was a nice girl once—well educated, you say? The employment of the word "proximity" rather suggests as much, though of course quite common people get hold of a long word which they work to death.'

'She was probably a criminal from her childhood. These people start very young,' said Branbury.

'I should not imagine so,' said the scientist quietly. 'I think you are underrating the demoralising power of our sex, Mr Branbury. If you investigate this matter to its beginnings, you will find that a man has had a very extraordinary influence upon this unfortunate woman. You will note from the evidence of your engineer that she protested that she was tired of the business, and you will probably find that behind all the calmness and cynicism, which is a mark of the habitual criminal, especially the woman criminal, there is a big aching heart, my friend. I am talking like a sentimentalist,' he laughed. 'Now let us get down to very unsentimental facts. Have you any data, any measurements, to give me?'

'I have brought her finger-prints and it is upon that subject that I want to see you. I shall ask you to be so kind as to go into the box as a witness for the prosecution.'

'To testify on the question of finger-prints?' he asked.

'Yes, my lord.'

'I do not like the publicity,' said Lord Exenham; 'but still if it is a public duty I will most certainly go into the box. Let me see the finger-prints.'

The detective took from his pocket a flat case which he opened, and took out first an enlarged photograph of the impression found on the scale and then an enlargement of the thumb-print which he had taken from the girl. The scientist compared them in silence, then he looked up with a frown.

'It is very extraordinary,' he said.

'Aren't they identical?' asked the detective quickly.

'Absolutely; there is no question about it,' said Lord Exenham; 'they are certainly identical, and yet—it is very extraordinary.'

He looked up at the detective again.

'I have a very excellent memory for thumb-prints; in fact, my mind is a big index of all the salient features of every thumb I have taken.'

He rose and went to one end of the room, unlocked a safe and extracted a book, which he opened on the table. Branbury, looking over his shoulder, saw that it was a sort of autograph album which was filled with finger-prints and beneath each finger-print was a name.

Lord Exenham turned the pages slowly and at last he stopped.

'Here we are,' he said. He picked up a magnifying glass and inspected one of the impressions, then he looked at the photograph and the enlargement of the girl's thumb-mark.

'This is amazing! Look for yourself, superintendent.'

The superintendent took the glass, looked and gasped—for the thumb- print in the book was identical with the thumb-prints of the criminal!

The same 'accidentals', the same 'whorl', the 'hooks' and 'deltas', even the clear heart-shaped core of the thumb-print was identical. He looked at the name beneath. It was 'Henry'.

'Who is this?' he asked.

'My son,' replied Lord Exenham simply, 'who has been dead these last six years and is buried in the parish church of this village.'

There was a deep silence.

'But, but,' stammered the detective, 'it is impossible. You know, my lord, it is impossible! There cannot be two thumb-prints alike. It would upset the whole system of criminal detection. If there is one weak link in the chain the whole process of identification by finger-prints goes by the board. Why, sir, it is your life's work—'

Lord Exenham was staring down at the print with pursed lips.

'Yes,' he said slowly, 'my life's work, but there it is.'

'Of course, it will be impossible to secure a conviction if this is made known?'

'It must be made known,' said his lordship quietly. 'I hardly know what to think or what to say. There is no doubt about that print,' he said, shaking his head. 'I know something of dactylography and I will swear that those three are identical.' Branbury shook his head helplessly.

'The whole system is based upon the belief that no two finger-prints can be exactly alike—this revolutionises the police systems of the world!' he said, almost in tones of awe as one who is confronted by a cataclysm.

He walked down to the station, declining the offer of Lord Exenham's motor-car, a bewildered and baffled man. He wanted to be alone to think it out, and he also desired to make a call at the parish church. Fortunately he found the church open and the sexton engaged in sweeping the floors.

'Oh, yes, sir, Mr Henry's buried here,' said the old man, and led him to a corner of the churchyard where a plain cross marked the resting-place of 'The Honourable Henry Curtice Exenham, only son of the Right Honourable the Lord Exenham, of this parish.'

'I knew him well, Mr Henry,' said the old man, 'a nice lad, but consumptive.'

Finding the detective interested, he took him to his cottage and showed him a portrait of the young man, a refined face bearing unmistakable evidence of the disease which had ended his young life.

Branbury returned to London and placed all the facts in front of his chief. Before he had left Lord Exenham had promised to forward the negative of the thumb-print, and until this arrived and was enlarged nothing could be done.

The negative reached Scotland Yard by special messenger on the following afternoon, and the three enlargements were viewed that night not only by the Commissioners, but by Dr Melsbury, Professor Caxton, Sir Jeremiah Findin (the Home Office Advisory Solicitor), and every expert on dactylography who could be reached at short notice.

'It didn't need enlarging,' said Sir Jeremiah, 'it is exactly the same print—what do you say, Caxton?'

'The impossible has happened,' he said; 'I think in fairness to our colleagues abroad we should notify all the police headquarters of this catastrophe—for catastrophe it is.'

Melsbury, stout and short of breath, was measuring the lineations with a tiny instrument and now sat up with a groan of despair.

'Bang goes the classifications of twenty years,' he wheezed. 'Think of the thousands of offices, and then imagine the millions of records that are so much wastepaper; it is hardly credible. Was his lordship upset, Branbury?'

'Yes—dazed would describe his condition.'

The Assistant-Commissioner was writing.

'How is this?' he asked at last, and read:

Very urgent. Lord Exenham has discovered an instance of dactylographical duplication. Two thumb-impressions, one of his dead son and one of known criminal, exactly correspond. Photographs will be sent you at earliest possible moment. Acknowledge to Scotland Yard.

'We cannot do less,' said Sir Jeremiah gloomily. 'As for California May—?'

'What do you advise?' asked the Commissioner.

'We shall offer no evidence unless we secure something outside of the finger-print.'

So it happened that, when 'Mabel Blixon' was called at the York Assizes, the Prosecutor rose and intimated that the Crown proposed to offer no evidence against her, and she was discharged with a curt nod from the judge.

In the meantime all the police world grew more and more frantic. From a dozen points of the compass officials were speeding to London. Urgent inquiries flashed from city to city—what was to be done? What steps were London, New York, Chicago, San Francisco, Paris, Melbourne taking?

On the twelfth day following the discharge and disappearance of Mabel Blixon' (for she had vanished in an inexplicable fashion) the chiefs of police of all the principal cities of the world received a cable:

DO NOT CHANGE FINGER-PRINT SYSTEM. IT IS INFALLIBLE. I HAVE AN EXPLANATION WHICH I WILL COMMUNICATE TO LONDON.

It was signed 'Exenham'.

The telegram reached Scotland Yard late in the afternoon, and Branbury left immediately for Exenham. What was the explanation? How could an explanation be possible?

To his annoyance he discovered that the train by which he travelled did not stop at Exenham Halt, and he was obliged to hire a fly at Burchester to drive back eight miles, and he did not reach the gates of the Hall until a quarter to ten that night.

Telling the driver to wait, he strode along the drive, across the park.

The house was in darkness, and when he rang the bell there was no answer. He rang again. It was too early for the household to have retired for the night, and, indeed, he remembered that Lord Exenham had confessed to being a very late worker.

Again he pressed the electric bell; then resting his hand upon the door he felt it give way.

He pushed open the door and walked in. The hall was in darkness, but he struck a match and closed the door behind him. To his surprise the lock did not catch, and he lit another match to discover the reason. The catch of the door was held back by a little lever. Perhaps, he thought, some servant had stolen forth surreptitiously and, being without a key, had chosen this simple method to secure his or her re-entrance.

He thought he heard voices and listened.

Lord Exenham's study was on the ground floor, opening from the big hall. The first and second doors to the right led, he judged, to a drawing-room, the third to the study—it was from this last chamber that the voices proceeded. He walked cautiously forward. If Lord Exenham was up and about, how dared the truant servant risk detection?

He heard the voices plainly now, Lord Exenham's calm monotone and another. The voice of the second man was shrill, angry and threatening.

'... my wife, I tell you, my wife. ... I told you what I'd do ... you tell me where ... don't move, you old dog ... put up your hands....'

Branbury waited to hear no more. In one stride he was at the door and had flung it open. As he did so, two shots, in rapid succession, stung his ear. The first came from near at hand, evidently from the man who stood with his back to the door supporting himself on the edge of the long table.

Branbury took in the scene at a glance—the swaying figure near him, the figure of Lord Exenham sprawling over the far end of the table, his pistol still poised. The detective's eyes came back to the stranger... wasp-waisted ... tall ... shrill of voice!

He remembered in a flash—then the man coughed and collapsed into Branbury's arms.

'I think he is dead,' said the even voice of Lord Exenham, and a glance at the ashen face of the stranger convinced the detective of the truth of this diagnosis.

'Lay him down and help me to the sofa—he got me, but he fired first,' said the scientist. 'I was afraid for a moment that he had only winged me, but I am happy to believe—thank you, Mr Branbury, I'm not in any great pain, which is a good sign.'

Branbury lifted the stricken man from the table and carried him to a settee in one of the window recesses. Lord Exenham's dark waistcoat was patched with blood.

'I'll get one of the servants to go for a doctor,' said Branbury.

Exenham smiled faintly.

'There are no servants,' he said. 'I packed them off to London, and no doctor could possibly reach me or, thank God, save my life. I am finished, but I have sufficient strength left to clear up a little mystery—you will find a bottle of brandy in the cupboard to the right of the fireplace.'

Branbury moistened the scientist's lips with the cordial, then dashed out into the park and raced back to the place where he had left the cab.

'Go into the village and find a doctor,' he said; 'there is a doctor's house near the station. If you can find the village constable bring him here. Knock up the cottagers and tell them I want men—Lord Exenham has been shot.'

He returned to find the wounded man still smiling to himself as at a pleasant memory.

'You have had your trouble for nothing, superintendent,' he said, 'and you have probably wasted very valuable time. Listen to what I have to say.'

He motioned to the brandy, and the officer assisted him to sip a little.

Presently the elder man spoke.

'I had two children, a boy and a girl. The boy, poor Harry, was a delicate lad and, as you know, died. The girl was of a different type. Self-willed, healthy and masterful. I'm afraid I did not give her the watchful care that it was my duty to provide. She was her own mistress and until she met Eric Gatterley she had her own way. Gatterley was, I knew, a bad lot. He had forged his father's name and was turned out. Later he stole and converted deeds from his employer's safe and a prosecution was only avoided by the efforts of his family. He was plausibly good-looking and, in spite of his effeminate voice and manner, a great favourite with women.'

He paused.

'You have never met Gatterley, have you?' he asked.

Branbury shook his head.

'If you will walk to the end of the table you will see him,' said Lord Exenham grimly. 'He is much less dangerous now than he ever was in his wicked life.'

He took another sip of brandy, this time without aid.

'I don't know how my girl got to know him, but the friendship was very far advanced when I discovered how matters stood and put my foot down. To my surprise she acquiesced meekly in the ban I pronounced, but I should have known that she was not to be turned from her purpose. One day she walked into this room and announced that she had married Eric. I think I must have gone mad. I ordered her and her husband from the house and refused to correspond with her. Gatterley was nonplussed. He had hoped that I would accept the fait accompli and receive him as my son-in-law. He probably expected to milk my fortune and was furious when he was undeceived. He bombarded me with letters, threatening, imploring, but generally demanding money. In the last letter I received from him he promised that I should pay dearly for my "insolence", and that since I had sent him a message that I would have nothing to do with an unconvicted thief he would make his wife worthy of a share in that title. He kept his promise.'

His voice sank and he did not speak again for a minute. Branbury knew now that the scientist's life was ebbing with every breath he drew.

Only the solemn 'tick-tick' of the clock on the mantelshelf broke the silence until Lord Exenham roused himself from his sad reverie.

'They went to America—Gatterley embezzled three thousand from his brother-in-law and had to fly. From time to time I tried to get into communication with my girl—once I succeeded in sending her a large sum of money to make her escape from the man, for I had heard through my agents that she was trying to get away. The money fell into Gatterley's hands and I heard no more until I read the account of the Halifax robbery and saw her portrait in the paper. I did not know until then that she had suffered imprisonment before or that she had earned her nick-name. I had a wild desire to save her—to fulfil that desire I determined to sacrifice everything.'

'But the finger-print?' asked Branbury eagerly.

'It was the recollection of that finger-print in a book in which I kept the impressions of a few friends and celebrities who came my way that decided me.'

He shifted himself with a little grimace of pain and smiled up at the detective.

'It was her thumb-print you saw,' he said. '"Henry" was short for "Henrietta". My poor boy was also Henry—but we called him "Snips"—you'll find his impression in the book. I determined upon the fraud— it was novel and convincing, since I, who advanced the proof, was the greatest authority on the subject of finger-prints. And it succeeded. My girl was met on leaving court by a trusted servant who knows the whole story, and she is now on her way to Australia with sufficient money to keep her in comfort.'

His voice was growing weaker; there were longer and longer pauses between his sentences, and Branbury strained his ears for the sound of the returning cab.

'Gatterley wrote threatening to expose me—the story of the similar finger-prints had reached the Press ... I invited him here ... to kill him ... fortunately ... able to destroy him ... perfectly legal....'

His voice sank to a tired murmur and he seemed to be sleeping. Then he slowly opened his eyes.

'Tell the truth about ... finger-prints ... great science ... infallible ... help my daughter ... if opportunity....'

He ceased to speak, and when a half-attired doctor came swiftly across the room ten minutes later there was no need for his services.

The Slip

The judge completed his address to the jury with a conventional peroration. It was Lent, and his robes were more sombre of hue than usual, yet he looked very young to be a judge of the King's Bench.

He had a small, sharp face, eyes deep-set and sparkling with good humour, nevertheless he was quick to lose his patience, easily irritated, ready with an acid tongue to correct, intolerant of humbug, infinitely just.

He finished his speech, leant back in his high chair with a quick jerk, and looked at the jury.

They were head to head, whispering decorously.

Then the foreman turned his face to the Bench.

'The jury wish to retire, my lord,' he said.

'Very well, very well,' said the judge, with indifference.

They stumbled down the two narrow wooden steps, these twelve good men, self-conscious of their importance. Each man gave a quick glance at the body of the court, taking in, first, the white-haired defendant, his black-rimmed monocle screwed into his right eye, his fresh-coloured face immovable and expressionless as that of a pink idol. He did not look toward them, because he did not care overmuch how the verdict went. Instinctively each man of the jury searched for the face of the plaintiff, but he had retired from the place he had occupied during the three days of the trial.

Ever a lover of an audience, he paced the great hall without in company with his counsel.

Reginald Saddin Sloe, Under-Secretary of State for Defence, needs no description of mine. Parry caricaturists have made the high forehead, the straight, thin nose, the plump, effeminate chin, and that up-brushed moustache of his, knowledgeable to more people in the world that will read this history. His eyes were blue, a thought too pale a blue to please most critics, his lips full. He smiled easily, showing two rows of even white teeth; but when he laughed he was disappointing, for his laugh was an explosive chuckle, and was without beauty.

If the jurymen did not see him they were perhaps a little relieved, for they had sat under his calm, benevolent gaze during the course of the case, until they had come to feel that they were rather the creatures of the plaintiff, his hired servants, holding their office at his will and on their good behaviour, rather than being the honest, independent men they were.

In the bare jury-room, with the door locked, and sworn custodian on the outside, they stood stretching their cramped limbs.

'Well, gentlemen,' said the foreman, with the show of geniality which his position demanded, 'what shall we say—plaintiff again?'

There was a reluctant murmur of assent, and a little man with a fringe of grey whisker shook his head so vigorously that his spectacles slipped from his nose.

'If there's justice in this land,' he said, settling his glasses right with one hand and groping vainly in his overcoat pocket for a handkerchief with the other, 'if the wells of truth ain't dried up, an'—an' bust, there ought to be some other verdict than one for the plaintiff.'

But the foreman was shaking his head, and he found imitators amongst his fellows.

'Weight of evidence, Mr Goss,' he said, 'weight of evidence—facts, facts, facts, my dear sir, not prejudice. We've got to go on evidence. The question is, did the Daily Journal libel Sloe when it said that he, being a Minister of the Crown, communicates Government secrets to a possible enemy?'

'Hear, hear,' muttered the rest of the jury.

'Did,' demanded the foreman, adopting a forensic tone, 'did the Daily Journal libel Sloe when it spoke of his being associated with a nest of international spies?'

'My own opinion,' said the dogged Mr Goss, planting himself more firmly in his chair, and looking up defiantly at his inquisitor, 'my own opinion is that it didn't—oh, I know all about the evidence, 'undreds of fellers ready to swear that he never did nothing!' In his indignation Mr Goss lost his grip on his mother tongue. 'Not a single witness to prove the Journal's words; 'undreds of witnesses to prove Sloe's an angel: Prime Minister, an' all the big pots.'

'Evidence, evidence,' murmured the foreman, tolerantly.

'An' don't you know that it's all true?' demanded little Mr Goss, jumping up and thumping the table indignantly; 'every word about Sloe is true! Ain't it the talk of London?'

'If it is,' replied the foreman, not without a touch of majestic pomposity, for he was a man of receptive mind, and the procedure of the court had impressed him, 'if all London knows, we must regard that as the direct result of the Journal's publication. Gentlemen, I think you will agree with me that a verdict for the plaintiff lies, and as to damages—'

'I don't agree!' stormed the little man, trembling with excitement; 'I will not be a party to allowing this blackguard to go to the world with a clean bill. Where are the Journal's witnesses?—spirited away?'

'Nonsense, Mr Goss!'

The foreman of the jury came down from his sublime heights and became humanly bad-tempered.

'Nonsense! Evidence—evidence—evidence! What's the good of your talking rubbish? Come here talking rot like that! Evidence! You can't get over the evidence. What was your oath? "And a true verdict given in accordance with the evidence, so help you God." Is that a fact, or isn't it? There's no doubt, there can be no reasonable doubt, that this is a case of spite—'

'But it ain't the Journal alone!' persisted the obstinate Mr Goss. 'All the papers have been doin' it. The Megaphone, The Telegram, The Newsletter, The Courier—his own party, Sloe's own party! We're wrong, we're wrong! I'm sure we're doin' wrong.' He wrung his hands and was on the verge of tears. 'But have it your own way. I'm done!'

And indeed he was, for he fell back in his chair physically exhausted with the strain.

'...We'll say ten thousand,' suggested the foreman, tentatively; 'it's a mere fleabite—eh, Mr Goss?'

'I don't care,' said the little man, listlessly; 'make it a million if you like.'

'We'll say ten thousand, gentlemen, eh?' The foreman had recovered his urbanity. 'After all, it was a bad libel...public man...might have ruined him, and all that. Ten thousand?'

He was ludicrously like an auctioneer as he peered expectantly round the faces at the table, as though in search of a higher bid. But no other suggestion came, and he rose, adjusted his tie, and gave the signal to the messenger of the court who waited outside the door.

The buzz of conversation died down as the twelve men filed into court, Mr Goss a listless old gentleman, with a fringe of grey whisker obtruding above his frayed collar.

'Gentlemen of the jury, have you agreed upon your verdict?'

'We have.'

'Do you find for the plaintiff or for the defendant?'

'For the plaintiff. We assess the damages at ten thousand pounds.'

'And is that the verdict of you all?'

Little Mr Goss strangled a protest in his throat, and nodded dumbly.

The white-haired man with the monocle rose and pulled down his waistcoat. There was a little smile on his hard mouth, a humorous glint in his eye. He lifted his immaculate silk hat from beneath the seat and carefully examined it. Then, with a slight inclination of his head to his solicitor, he walked out of court.

In the great hall he came face to face with his enemy, and for a second or so they stood looking at one another, the Under-Secretary showing his white teeth in undisguised triumph, the newspaper proprietor with his grim little shadow of a smile and his immovable, black-rimmed monocle.

'Fortunes of war, Sir Francis,' said Sloe, pleasantly.

The other man nodded, a quick jerk of a nod.

'I suppose anything I say now will be taken down as evidence and used against me?' he smiled.

'Not at all, Sir Francis,' said the Minister; 'we are not vindictive.' He put out his hand. 'I think you are quite at liberty to add any comment you wish.'

'I will only say this,' said the newspaper proprietor, 'that for the moment you are too clever for us. We believe, indeed we know, that you are something worse than a traitor; but you are genius enough to hide your tracks so well that, unless we had the aid of the Government, which we never have had, there is no hope of detecting you—at present,' he added.

Sloe laughed a noiseless little chuckle of sheer delight.

'I cannot dissipate your illusions, so it is rather useless to protest. Is that all you have to say?'

'Only this,' said Sir Francis Wilton, slowly, 'the cleverest men make a slip. It is the history of all—' he paused—'shall I say clever men? Some stupid, foolish blunder, which undoes all the careful and well-arranged plans of years. It is the Nemesis that waits upon the super-criminal. Good-morning.'

Sloe was still smiling as he made an elaborate bow. He exchanged a few words with his solicitor, congratulated his counsel, and stepped into his car.

A quarter of an hour later he was its his handsome flat at Albert Gate. Save for his valet it was empty, and him he dispatched upon a message to Whitehall. He passed into his study, closed and locked the door behind him, and drew a heavy silken curtain across the door to afford him even greater security.

He took a bunch of keys from his pocket, pulled back the panel which hid the safe let in the wall, and opened the heavy steel door. He unlocked a drawer, and from this extracted a large envelope. He carried it to the writing-table, took from the writing-desk an empty parchment envelope, and put it by his side. Then he examined the contents of the dossier he had taken from the safe. Everything was there. The thin, paper-covered code-book, the correspondence which had passed between him and von Schroeder, the duplicate plans of the Harwich defences, the mobilization mine-field chart, quite sufficient indeed to have made the name of Reginald Sloe execrated, and to have brought a brilliant Under-Secretary to a felon's cell.

He laughed as he turned them over one by one, checking them carefully before he inserted them in the parchment envelope.

You are a little too dangerous,' he said, playfully; 'what would not my friend Sir Francis give for these? Back you go to Holland. Wilton has scared me.'

Wilton was the most dangerous of all. He had no difficulty in securing apologies from the other papers who had printed stories from their Amsterdam correspondents, but Wilton had twice fought an action, had twice lost; but with each case the mud had stuck.

Reginald Sloe was a bold man and conscienceless. He could walk into a witness-box and lie so perfectly that he deceived himself. But the Journal case had shaken him. He would seal up the envelope and trust it to that safest of repositories, the general post. The packet should go to Herr von Schroeder, and nobody would be any the wiser. He was thinking of Francis Wilton as he licked down the flap. He was smiling over his enemy's discomfiture as he poured out the three little pools of sealing-wax and pressed down the seal of his department. He was still smiling when he wrote the address.

Wilton was in his thoughts all the way between the flat and the General Post Office, and when the great envelope finally disappeared from sight in the big box marked 'Foreign Correspondence', the picture of the grey-haired editor was still in his mind.

One little slip—the cleverest make them, he thought. Somehow he knew that the journalist was right. Very well, then; there should be no opportunities for such a slip. Schroeder must send him nothing more. No further communications must pass.

He was cheerful for the rest of the day; went to the House in the happiest frame of mind, and received the congratulations of his colleagues; retired that night with a sense of relief which had not been his for weeks; and was humming a tune at his breakfast the next morning, when Superintendent Maguires, of Scotland Yard, came into his room and arrested him.

For the envelope he had sent away had been addressed mechanically.

'Sir Francis Wilton,
'Editor of the Daily Journal,
'Fleet Street.'

A Raid on a Gambling Hell

I have had to deal with all classes of society, high and low, rich and poor, and number amongst clients several millionaires, crooks, peers and peeresses, and servant girls. It is my boast that nothing surprises me, yet I must confess feeling a mild tinge of excitement at receiving, on the letter-head of the Ministry of the Interior, a request that I would call at eleven o'clock upon Mr. George Tresham, the Minister in question.

The Right Honourable George Tresham was a name to conjure with on the day I received that summons. A comparatively young man who had won his way to the foremost Cabinet rank by sheer ability and courage, he had as solid a following as any Minister in the House.

'I have sent for you, Dixon,' he said, 'on a very delicate private matter. A matter,' he went on, 'which affects my personal honour—indeed, affects my whole future career.'

Motioning me to a chair, he began the narrative which is set down below. Of course, I am not giving the real names of persons and places.

George Tresham, in addition to being a popular statesman, was something of a man about town. He had a host of friends, mostly younger than himself, and his interest in the theatre had extended to the writing of a four-act drama, which had been produced with moderate success in the West End. It was during his brief incursion into the realms of dramatic authorship that he made the acquaintance of Bart Philipson—the Honourable Bartholomew Philipson—who, at the time this narrative was told me, had succeeded to his father's very small and very heavily encumbered estate as Lord Colesun.

Bart Philipson, as he was then, had an interest in the theatre wherein Mr. Tresham's play was produced.

The two became fast friends, for George Tresham was a large-hearted, lovable soul, who was attracted rather than repelled by the other's cynicism and worldliness. Tresham was, of course, enormously wealthy.

The two friends were talking at their club one night, and the conversation drifted round to gambling hells. Bart gave a very vivid word-picture of one he had visited in London, and Tresham expressed his surprise that such places existed, and also asked his friend to take him to see one some night.

About a month later, on a Thursday evening, when Tresham had finished his solitary dinner, the telephone bell rang, and his butler told him that Lord Colesun was on the telephone.

'I say,' said Bart's voice, 'are you still keen on seeing one of those places we were speaking about the other night?'

'Rather!' said Tresham, who was bored, and welcomed any diversion.

'Well, there's a new place opened in Montacute Square,' said Bart's voice. 'I don't know very much about it, except that I've got the password and the right of entrée for a friend. I am told it is unique in many respects.'

'All right. I'll come along.'

Tresham ordered his car, picked up Bart, and dismissed the car at the corner of Montacute Square. The two walked on. It was a foggy night, but Bart knew the way.

'Here we are,' he said, and, ascending a short flight of broad steps, he knocked in a peculiar manner on the door.

It was opened by a servant in quiet livery, and after a glance at Bart the two were passed into a hall which was dimly lighted and escorted up a stairway to a landing above. A pair of folding doors confronted them. On this the servant knocked. The door opened a few inches, and a keen eye scrutinised the pair.

'All right; come in, gentlemen,' said the owner of the eye, and they were admitted into a large saloon, blazing with light and richly furnished.

But it was not the appointments which made Tresham stare. It was not even the green table in the centre of the room, around which a dozen men were playing. It was the other questionable occupants. Men and women, the latter in wildly extravagant costumes, were sitting at little tables, taking no notice of the players. They all had the appearance of being under the influence of drink, and very far under at that.

'How perfectly beastly!' Tresham said. 'A perfect saturnalia! Let us get out of this, Bart.'

'I quite agree,' said the phlegmatic Lord Colesun. He was turning to the door, when it burst open, and a wild-eyed servant dashed in.

'The police! The police!' he gasped, and had hardly got the words out of his mouth when two or three policemen burst into the room after an inspector, and were followed by a dozen men in plain clothes. Immediately began a stampede, a kicking over of tables, a screaming of women, a shouting of men. Somebody cried, 'Put out the lights.' One man attempted to unshutter the window, and was pulled back by a constable, and in the end the inspector made his voice heard.

'Ladies and gentlemen,' he said, 'you will all consider yourselves under arrest. I shall take you to Bow Street Police Station.'

'My God! What shall I do?' said Tresham. 'It is ruin, Bart.'

'Keep quiet,' said Bart in a low voice. 'I'll see what I can do.'

He went across to the inspector, and at first the officer would have nothing to say to him. Then Bart said something in a low voice, and the two men stepped aside into a corner of the room, and for a few moments conversed together. Presently Bart strode back to Tresham.

'A policeman will take us out of the door,' he said. 'I've squared him.'

A constable approached and the two men were pushed unceremoniously on to the hall landing and escorted down the stairs.

'All right,' said Bart to the constable and slipped something into his hand.

'Hold hard, sir,' said the policeman, 'I seem to know that gentleman's face.'

'Never mind what you know,' said Bart.

'It's all right, sir. I hope there's no offence,' said the policeman, 'but if that isn't Mr. Tresham, I'm a Dutchman.'

Tresham looked at the man, but could not see his face. He noted, however, that one of his front teeth was broken. In a few moments they were out in the street, Bart cursing himself for having led his friend into such a mess. Tresham stopped him.

'Don't be a fool, Bart,' he said, 'it was my own stupid curiosity which is entirely responsible. What did you say to the inspector fellow?'

'I said a thousand pounds,' said Bart briefly, 'It was the only argument I could think of.'

'Of course I'll pay that,' said Tresham. 'In fact, it's cheap at the price. What about that infernal policeman? Do you think he'll talk?'

'I'll have to go back and see him,' said Bart. 'Otherwise, I don't think there's anybody there who recognised you, not even the inspector.'

George Tresham got home at 11.30, spent a restless night, and when, passing along Whitehall the next afternoon, he saw on the newspaper placards the announcement of a gambling raid, his heart beat faster. Fortunately it was scrappy, merely mentioning the fact that a raid had been made on a house in Montacute Square, that a certain number of people had been arrested, the proprietor had been fined and imprisoned, and that two servants who assisted in the conduct of the house had also been sent to prison. There was no mention of the unpleasant things he had seen; and that afternoon, when Bart came by appointment, the reason was explained.

'I saw the inspector again this morning,' he said, 'and I asked him to keep that part of it quiet, in case it ever came out that I was there. But I'm afraid we're going to have trouble with the policeman,' he went on, shaking his head. 'He's a man named Bowker, a shrewd and unscrupulous fellow, who has been in trouble before, and apparently has already announced his intention of resigning from the force to live upon a private income.'

'What does he mean by that?'

'He means you are the private income, I am afraid.' said Bart grimly.

'Blackmail?' demanded Tresham.

'That's what it amounts to,' said Bart.

'This is dreadful,' said Tresham with a despairing gesture. 'Have you seen this policeman?'

'That's what it amounts to,' said Bart.

'I've just come from him,' said Bart. 'I've found his address—he lives in Bayswater—and made a call. As I feared, he intends making us pay.'

'Did he mention a figure?'

'He did,' said Bart. 'He asked for fifty thousand pounds!'

'Fifty thousand pounds!' Even Tresham was startled.

'Seventy really,' said Bart. 'Fifty from you and twenty from me. Heaven knows where I'm going to get my twenty from.'

Tresham thought for a while.

'When does he want his answer?' he demanded.

'Tomorrow evening at the latest,' said Lord Colesun. 'I have an appointment to meet him on Hammersmith Broadway.'

It was after his friend's departure that Mr. Tresham sat down and wrote the letter that brought me to his study.

I listened in silence and sympathy to the narrative.

'Have you told Lord Colesun that you have sent for me?' I asked.

He shook his head.

'No,' he replied; 'but, of course, I shall tell him.'

'I would rather you didn't,' said I. 'I prefer working under one pair of eyes and with only one set of theories to combat.'

'Namely, mine?' he smiled faintly.

'Namely, yours, sir,' I said. 'You can afford to pay fifty thousand pounds, although I don't suppose anybody can afford to part with such an enormous sum. But Lord Colesun—is it humanly possible that he can pay?'

The Minister shook his head.

'Did he give you the address of the policeman?' I asked.

'No; it is somewhere in Bayswater, but he is meeting him tonight at Hammersmith. You will have to work with Lord Colesun, because he knows the man, and will be able to introduce you if necessary,' he said.

'What do you want me to do?' I asked.

The Minister hesitated.

'Well, I hardly know, except that I should like you to see the fellow and beat his price down. Maybe you could scare him?*

I shook my head.

'That kind of man isn't easily scared,' said I. 'He is evidently a thoroughly bad lot, and, being a policeman or an ex-policeman, as he will be in a day or two, he knows the law just as well as I, and he would be a difficult man to bluff. Now, if you'll be advised by me, Mr. Tresham, you will not say a word to Lord Colesun as to having seen or employed me.'

'But what can you do?' he asked. 'You do not even know the policeman's address.'

'I'll make a few inquiries which will help me to clear up the mystery of the drunken people.'

'Mystery?' he said. 'There was no mystery about it; they were there.'

'Exactly,' said I with a smile: 'but that is the mystery. Don't you realise, Mr. Tresham, that in gaming houses drunkenness is as rare as at a revival meeting?'

I thereupon left him and pursued my investigation.

Scotland Yard very kindly gave me a few particulars, and the Home Office the necessary permission to see the proprietor of the raided gambling-house. He was in Wandsworth Gaol, and to Wandsworth I drove, handed in my order, and was taken to where a stout, elderly man sat on the edge of his seat.

'I want to talk to you about this raid of yours,' said I. 'How did they come to catch you?'

'How? Why, I was given away,' he said vehemently, 'and what's more, I know the man that gave me away.'

'Who was it?' I asked.

'You find out,' he snapped. 'I name no names; I keep my opinions to myself. I was running one of the quietest, best-conducted little joints in London, and it's a shame they couldn't leave me alone.'

'I like your idea of well-conducted little joints,' said I, and in a few brief words I gave him my own opinion of the class of establishment he kept.

'That's a lie,' he said. 'If there were a lot of lushers lying about don't you think the police would have brought it out?

'Anyway, I'm glad they raided me when they did, if they were going to raid at all,' he went on. 'If they'd come a couple of hours later we should have been in full swing. As it was, they caught a few. The police messed it, as they mess everything. Fancy raiding a gaming house at half-past nine at night!' he said contemptuously. 'You're a split, aren't you?'

'I am a sort of detective,' I admitted.

'Well, don't think I've got anything against the police, because I haven't,' he said. 'Inspector Ericson was decent to me, and I don't suppose he'd have raided me, if that swine hadn't given me away. I'll "Bart" him when I come out.'

'What name was that?' I said quickly.

'Never mind,' he replied evasively, and try as I did, he could not be induced to say any more.

Now, Inspector Ericson is one of the straightest men in London. No Robespierre was more incorruptible. He was certainly not the kind of man who would accept a thousand pounds to allow a detected gambler to go scot free.

Ericson was not at the station when I called, and I took the liberty of driving over to his house, and found him preparing to go on night duty.

'I wanted to see you, inspector, about the raid you made the other night.'

'Oh, did you?' he said, with his hard little smile.

'When you made the raid why did you choose half-past nine?'

'Well, the raid was made in accordance with instructions we received from headquarters. The gentleman who gave the house away told us that at half-past nine it was crowded, and, what's more, he had arranged with the doorkeeper to let us in at that hour.'

'Another question, Ericson. When you made the raid, did anybody offer you a thousand pounds to let them out?'

'I think not. Otherwise it would have been as good as paying me to put them in!' he said.

'I happen to know,' said I, 'that the gentleman who gave you the information which led to the raid was Lord Colesun.'

'You do, do you?' said he. 'Ah, well, you know a lot!'

'Well, I won't ask you whether it was he or somebody else,' said I. 'But tell me this—was your informant present when the raid was made?'

'I can answer you very emphatically that he was not,' replied Ericson.

'Just one more question, Inspector. Do you know whether there are any other gambling houses in Montacute Square?'

'I can tell you that there are not,' said the inspector, 'it is funny you should ask that. It was the same question asked by one of my detective-sergeants who was watching the place we raided. He reported that a lot of people had gone in to No. 27. The house we raided was No.43, farther along. He went over to make an inquiry, but found there was a fancy-dress ball on or something. In fact, he mistook a dressed-up policeman, as he thought, who was going into the house as a real one.'

'Thank you, that's all I want to know,' said I, and went back to the office to get the report of my assistants, who had spent that afternoon making inquiries in knowledgeable circles in the city.

Their reports were very satisfactory from my point of view, and I was in the midst of reading them when Mr. Tresham rang through and asked me to come and see him.

'I hope I haven't annoyed you, Mr. Dixon, but I have had to tell Lord Colesun. I thought it was hardly fair to him. Will you come over?'

'Is he with you?' I asked.

'He is with me now.'

I gathered up the reports and read the last two on my way to Whitehall. Lord Colesun I had not met before.

He shook hands with me warmly on my introduction.

'Glad to meet you, Mr. Dixon. I have heard about you, and I am extremely glad that my friend Mr. Tresham has called you in. I was a little ratty when I heard in the first place, but since then I agree that it was wise to take professional advice. Mr. Tresham and I have been talking the matter over, and we have decided that the best thing to do is to pay this infernal policeman and let the matter rest.'

'I think it is the best thing to do,' broke in Mr. Tresham. 'I did have a wild idea that it would be better if you met the policeman, but on consideration I have decided that Bart—Lord Colesun—should carry the thing through himself.'

'I never expected to meet this policeman,' said I. 'At least, not in his role as a policeman. You said, Mr. Tresham, that although you did not see the policeman's face you noticed that he had one of his front teeth broken.'

Mr. Tresham nodded. I turned to Lord Colesun.

'May I ask you,' I said, 'if you know any person who has a front tooth broken?'

'I probably know several. I don't notice the teeth of policemen, however.'

'I am not talking about policemen,' I insisted. 'Do you know any other person with a broken front tooth?'

I had seen the young man's face change, and now he picked up his hat from a settee and walked towards the door.

'I'd like you to excuse me for a little while; I'm not feeling very well,' he said in a low voice.

'Wait!' said I, 'I have to finish my story.'

'Then you'll finish it alone,' snarled the man at the door, and went out, slamming it behind him.

The Minister looked at me in bewilderment.

'What does it all mean.'

'It means this,' said I. 'Your friend Lord Colesun has for months been on the verge of bankruptcy. Moreover, he has been taking funds from a company with which he is connected, which must be made good by tomorrow morning.'

'Good God! You don't suggest—' he began.

'I suggest that the gambling hell and the supposed police raid were got up for your special benefit. The gamblers and the police were members of a provincial touring company, who were brought to London to play their part by Lord Colesun, who told them that he was having a joke on one of his friends. The house was hired furnished—'

'But why the drunkenness?' asked Mr.Tresham.

'That was intended to make you all the more disgusted and all the more anxious to keep your name out of the case. To make the deception seem more real, your friend arranged for a gaming club, which undoubtedly existed in Montacute Square, to be raided the same night—as a matter of fact, an hour and a half before the sham raid was made. The policeman with the broken tooth was Lord Colesun's valet.'

'Then you suggest,' said Mr. Tresham in a low voice, 'that Bart was blackmailing me, and that the fifty thousand pounds was for himself?'

'I not only suggest that, but I advance it as a fact,' said I. 'The valet is a man who has been hand-in-glove with his Lordship in every dirty piece of business in which he has been engaged. Your friend arranged for a raid on a genuine gaming club in order that you should be able to read something in the next day's paper. The sham police who "raided" were in one of the rooms downstairs waiting until you were safely inside the saloon.'

The Minister sat at his desk, his head on his hands. At last he rose.

'Well, Mr. Dixon,' he said with a smile, 'you have saved me fifty thousand pounds, but you have cost me a very dear illusion.'

'You will not prosecute, of course?' said I.

He shook his head.

'If there is any of his father's spirit in the man, there will be no necessity for a prosecution,' he said quietly.

Tresham was right as it happened, for the first announcement I read when I opened my paper the following morning was that Lord Colesun had shot himself.

If—?

The war had soured Hector Smith. It had drawn a line between comparative youth and comparative middle-age. It had burst inconveniently, as wars have a habit of bursting, upon more than one half-matured scheme of his, and had scattered them to bits and left him the poorer. To be exact, it had left Mary the poorer, because it was Mary's money that went, of which fact it had become a habit of hers to remind him.

But more souring, bits of boys, the merest urchins, to be patronized or ignored in the old days, had obtruded themselves upon his and the public's attentions. The balance of life was over-set. The inconsiderable factors (in which category he included these boys who now strutted consciously be-ribboned through his world) had grown to such importance that they overshadowed the real big things of life, such as his handicap at golf, his bridge hands, the remarkable poverty of intelligence on the part of his partners, and the like.

There was a time when Arthur, for example, would have been carried to the seventh heaven by a timely half-sovereign, and would have run his long legs off in his haste to reach the confectioner's before the cream buns were sold. Now Arthur was a straight-limbed youth with "wings," and a record of good service in France.

And Arthur and Mary—

Pshaw! It was absurd! Why, he remembered this dirty little kid when he was so high! Yet, it was a fact that Mary spent most of her time with Arthur, raved about his dancing, his beautiful manners, his perfect sympathy. Pshaw!

Hector Smith cursed the war that forced him to listen to gruesome stories in which he was not interested.

He opened the drawing-room door and stalked in, then stopped with a little grimace. The inevitable Arthur was there, and the inevitable Arthur with an embarrassed giggle made his escape with a mumbled reference to the weather. As for Mary, she looked too good to be true.

"Hasn't that bird got a perch of his own?" snarled Hector.

"How can you speak of a man who has been wounded—?" began his indignant partner.

Mr. Smith laughed contemptuously.

"Wounded! The first time he tried to fly he crashed, and the second time he tried to fly he crashed, and the third time he tried to fly he crashed!"

She tossed her head.

"I'd like to see you do it!"

Mr. Smith shrugged.

"Oh, I know it's a mistake to talk disrespectfully of your hero," he sneered.

He was not feeling at his brightest.

"What do you mean?" she demanded with ominous calm.

"I mean, I'm fed up, that's what I mean," he snapped, and she flamed round on him.

"And so am I!" she cried. "You're vulgar and stupid and tyrannical. The life I've lived with you is abominable. When I married you I had money—"

He bowed.

"That's right," he said, encouragingly, "throw that in my face! Didn't I invest it for you?" It was an unfortunate question.

"Yes, you did," she said, bitterly. "You put it into a luminous sign business. Luminous signs! And a month after war was declared! And the only thing you could get out of showing a luminous sign was six months' imprisonment!"

"How did I know there was going to be a war?" asked the exasperated man.

"You might have guessed it," she replied, illogically.

"Could I guess that London was to be plunged in darkness? I did my best. I should have made a million out of that fuse factory I started this year—"

"Yes, if it hadn't been for the armistice," she scoffed.

"How did I know there was going to be peace?" he roared.

She flounced past him on her way to the door.

"Oh, you never know anything!"

"There's one thing I know," he shouted after her.

"What's that?"

"One of these fine days I'll run away to America!" Her scornful laugh came back through the slammed door. He threw himself upon the settee. The money was gone and the wife remained. That was his luck. If it had been the other way about—! If only it had been the other way about! If he could only live the years over again! If he could only be five years younger and knew what he knew!

He sat staring at the newspaper in his hand. There was a critique of a new play, a fairy play.

Bah! Fairies were nonsense!

He laid the newspaper down on his knees.

But suppose there were such things as fairies, and suppose they moved about this prosaic, industrialized world as in the old days they moved through the woodland glebes; suppose by a wave of a magic wand a man could be transplanted back, back, back; and suppose that it were possible that the clock should be put back, and one had consciousness of all the things that were going to happen, the horses that were going to win races, the stocks which were going to rise, all the great events which must occur!

He heaved a deep sigh and looked up. He half-rose from the couch, for there before him, a bright and radiant figure in the dusky room, stood a brilliant presence. He knew it was a fairy because it was dressed as fairies should be dressed, and bemuse she was bathed in a flood of silvery light which seemed to come from nowhere in particular. The little hands grasped a wand which twinkled and glittered with light.

Recovering from his initial astonishment he looked at her aappraisingly. He felt it would be undignified and ill-bred to regard her as a phenomenon.

"Hector Smith," said a sweet, low voice,

"I am your fairy godmother!"

"Oh, yes." said Hector Smith, politely.

"You have expressed a wish to be five years younger. Be happy, for to-morrow you will awake in 1914."

"Eh?" said Hector, sitting up. "I say, do you really mean that?"

She inclined her head.

"Wait a moment," said Hector, eagerly. "I must be the only one who knows it. D'ye understand? Because if everybody else knows it I shall be in the cart again."

She raised her wand and waved it slowly above his head.

"I must be the only one who knows that there's going to be a war and all that sort of thing," said Hector, drowsily. A sense of languor was rapidly overcoming him. "I don't want...."

His head fell on his chest.

He did not know how long he had slept when he awoke with a jerk. He had a confused dream in which figured fairies and brilliant wands, and low, sweet voices mingled, and then he remembered that he had to see Tomkins who was liquidating his ill-fated fuse factory. He went to the study and 'phoned Tomkins, but, amazingly enough, Tomkins was not on the 'phone. He asked Exchange to connect him with Smith's Patent Fuse Factory, but Exchange was ignorant that such a place had ever existed.

"The telephone service," said Hector Smith, as be hung up the receiver, "is becoming more and more abominable."

He decided to write to the newspapers on the subject. He paused outside the drawing-room door, for he heard his wife moving about inside, and it was necessary to brace himself up for the ordeal. He was a little scared of Mary in her tantrums, and more scared that his apprehension should be known to her. But the girl who came across the room to meet him had no frown, no reproaches. She was one beaming smile, and she ran towards him and laid her hands upon his shoulders.

"Dearie!" she kissed him, ecstatically: then noting the gloom in his face, "darling, whatever is the matter?"

"Matter?" he answered, suspiciously. "What's that you did? What's the matter with you?"

She looked at him in wonder.

"Nothing is the matter with me. I just kissed you, that's all."

He heaved a sigh. How did she know he had received his directors' cheque that day?

"How much do you want?" he asked, with resignation.

"Naughty boy, why do you say that?" she pouted. "Don't you love your diddlelums any more?"

He stared at her.

"Look here. What's up?" he asked, desperately. "I'll buy it! What's wrong with you?"

"Wrong?"

She was frankly astonished.

"Everything has gone wrong to-day," he growled. "I went to call up that fellow about the fuses—"

She frowned.

"Fuses? What are fuses?"

His suspicions returned. "Don't pull my leg," he said, coldly. "I'm not in a mood for it. Try it on the other fellow."

"What other-fellow?" He jerked his head to the door.

"He was heme just now. I heard his voice."

A smile of understanding dawned on her face.

"Who, little Arthur?"

"Yes, little Arthur," he snarled, "the little hero!"

"Don't be silly, Hector," she laughed.

"Arthur a hero!"

His rising wrath moderated. Evidently what he had said to her had done some good. Still suspicious, and with a horrid sense of unreality, he slipped his arm about her waist and led her to the couch. It was all unreal and unexpected, he thought, as her golden head rested on his shoulder.

"It's a long time since we did this," he said. "It reminds me of the raid nights."

She straightened herself up.

"The what nights?"

"The raid nights."

She laughed. Hector in the full ardour of that period which was neither youth nor middle-age, had been a tempestuous lover.

"Dear, you use such queer expressions!"

"Do you remember the siren?" he asked, after a pause, and her head nodded vigorously.

"Yes, the cat—but I got you away from her."

"And how we used to go down into the cellar?" he mused. It seemed a thousand years ago. She straightened up. It was she who was suspicion.

"We never did," she protested. "Really, Hector! I hope you're not thinking of somebody else?"

Before he could answer Jane came in, and Jane, curiously enough, looked much younger.

"Will there be three to dinner, madam?" asked the maid.

Mary nodded.

"Who is the third?" demanded Mr. Smith.

"Oh, no one," said his wife, airily. "I asked Arthur to stay."

He sprang to his feet.

"Arthur! Confound the fellow, hasn't he gone? I won't have him. Do you understand. Marv. I-won't-have-him!"

Again the look of blank astonishment on her face.

"But why not?"

"He's such a nice little gentleman, sir," pleaded Jane. "He sat on my knee and told me such funny stories."

Hector glared from the maid to his wife.

"There you are!" he said, triumphantly. "That's the sort of fellow he is! Sits on her knee and tells her funny stories!"

To his amazement she laughed.

"It's not worth while getting angry—he can dine in the kitchen."

"In the kitchen!"

"Of course, he doesn't care," Mary went on, calmly, "so long as he goes to the White City."

"With whom?"

"Well, I'll take him," said Mary, indifferently. "I rather like the Roly-Poly and the Wiggle-Wag."

With a mighty effort Mr. Smith controlled himself.

"You can't go to the White City. It's been requisitioned by the Government four years ago," he said. "The White City is closed, I tell you. It's where the C3 men get their A1 gratuity—everybody knows that."

There was a strained silence, during which Jane tip-toed from the room.

Hector saw something in his wife's eyes that looked like fear, and failed to diagnose its cause.

"I'm sorry I lost my temper," he said, penitently; "the fact is I'm jealous."

The fear was replaced by a gleam of interest.

"Jealous? Of whom?"

He made a little gesture to cover his discomfort.

"Of you—and Arthur."

"But you're mad," she gasped; "at his age—"

"At his age." said Mr. Smith, icily, "I had been thrown out of the Empire twice."

He did not explain the degree of worldliness which this experience implied, but he left her to gather that it represented a particularly lurid form of precocity.

"I don't understand you to-night," she said, shaking her head.

"I don't understand myself," said Mr. Smith, rising. "I think I'll run down to the club, I promised to meet an ace."

"An ace? I thought you'd given up cards."

"You don't understand me—this fellow brought down thirty."

"Thirty what?"

"Boche."

"It isn't 'bosh'!" she exploded. "How did he bring them down?"

Hector groaned.

"He got on their tails and crashed them," he explained, patiently.

She was shocked.

"Poor things! I suppose they broke quite easily?" she asked.

He looked at her.

"I don't know what you are talking about," he said, irritably. "I am speaking about a fellow who has been 'mentioned' six times."

She shook her head.

"This is the first time you have mentioned him to me," she said; "what has he done?"

"Done? Why, in the early days before he started flipping, he took a pill-box all by himself!"

Her mouth opened.

"A whole box?" she gasped.

"You see," he explained, "he was in a tank, and when they went over the top—"

"Over the top of the tank?" she asked, hazily.

"No, the tank went over the top and a minnie dropped in front of him."

She was interested again.

"Poor girl," she said, sympathetically, "and did he help her up?"

"No; you see, a dying pig burst just behind him."

"But what did he do with Minnie?" she demanded.

She could not grapple with pigs that flew, but Minnie was someone tangible.

"Oh, she got him in the leg," he stated, carelessly.

She was grave now.

"I see, she wasn't a lady?"

"Of course she wasn't a lady," he wailed.

"I have told you it wasn't a lady! It was a minenwerfer."

She did not want to hear about Miss Werfer or even of a low person to whom he made glib reference—a Miss Emma Gee. This friend of her husband's seemed to have low tastes. He crashed people, he got on their tails.

"And Big Bertha—" Hector was saying when she stopped him.

"I don't think I want to meet your friend," she said, and made for the door.

He didn't understand her. Usually she was as full of the jargon of the war as the most ardent subaltern. Now she professed ignorance and demanded an elucidation of the most commonplace phrase.

He was pondering on this fact when the maid came into the room. She stood nervously waiting, and Hector guessed her errand.

"Well?" he growled.

"I-I thought I would ask you, sir," she faltered; "I was going to ask the mistress if-if she would give me a little rise."

"A rise again!" he groaned. This was the third or was it the fourth time...?

"But, sir?"

"Now listen to me," he said, severely, "I know that living is expensive, and coals are dear, and I am willing to give you another rise. But this must be the very last time. You can have five pounds a month, but not a penny more."

She did not swoon. She was too well-bred a servant.

"Five pounds a month! Oh, thank you, master, thank you! Oh, you are most good—"she grew incoherent.

Hector raised his eyebrows. He thought she was unusually grateful. His wife returned at that moment to hear his news.

"By the way, dear, I've just raised Jane's wages."

Usually she objected to his interfering in her domestic affairs, but now she was most amiable.

"I promised her I would—she seems a nice girl."

"Yes," said Hector. "I'm giving her five pounds a month."

His wife grasped a chair for support.

"Are you mad?" She beckoned Jane, for her earlier suspicions were now certainties.

"Fetch a doctor," she said, under her breath. "The master isn't well. I only pay her eighteen pounds a year."

She tried to say this in a light conversational tone, but her voice shook.

"You only—?" Something was very wrong, and he called the maid to him. "Ask Dr. Sawyer to step round. Mrs. Smith isn't quite herself," he said.

"Get Dr. Thomas." demanded Mary, sharply.

Thomas! Thomas was in Mesopotamia! It was clear now. The worry of the past years had turned her brain. It was a flattering explanation for the preference she had lately shown to Arthur. They watched one another apprehensively after the girl had gone, then:—

"Feel better, ducky?" he asked, huskily.

"Has that nasty wuzzy feeling gone, lovey?" her voice was a nervous squeak.

Dr. Thomas had the flat opposite, and Dr. Thomas was coming out of his flat when the frightened maid had literally flung herself upon him.

"They're both mad," she babbled, and the startled doctor followed her to where two people, each standing at the extreme end of a long drawing-room, were watching one another in silence. Hector saw him and uttered an exclamation of astonishment.

"By Jove. I thought you were in Bagdad?"

The doctor laid his soothing hand on the other's shoulder.

"Of course—Bagdad! Ah, that's the place—we'll soon put you right, old man."

Ignoring the implication that he wasn't right, Mr. Smith whispered something in the other's ear.

"Of course she is," replied Thomas, indulgently, and caught Mary's eye and Mary's significant signal.

It was at that moment that Arthur came in—Arthur in his Eton suit, with his cherubic face stained with jam. Hector looked at him and his jaw dropped.

"What the devil have you dressed like this for?" he demanded.

"Because I'm going to school, Mr. Smith."

"To school? How old are you?"

"Fourteen—nearly."

"Fourteen!" repeated Hector, hollowly.

"Is it possible—?"

On Mary's desk was a calendar and to this he walked.

"Nineteen fourteen! Mary, I understand all. I will explain. You're not mad—it was the fairy—who put back the clock!—my wish was granted!"

The doctor looked at Mary and Mary looked at the doctor. "I'm going to prophesy," Hector went on, excitedly. "We are going to war! The Kaiser will abdicate! The British Army will be seven millions strong! We shall win the war, thanks to Beatty, Haig, and Foch!"

He saw the round face of Arthur and—smack! Arthur sprawled on the door, blubbering.

"Why did you do that?" asked the terrified Mary.

"He's going to cause me a lot of trouble," said Hector, prophetically

Mr. Miller and the Kaiser

Against the day when explorers and archaeologists rake over the junk of Britain's forgotten cities, as today they take the mounds where Tarquin lorded it, and reconstruct Etruscan history from her crockery-ware, against such a day when paper and parchment and even sheep-skins have perished with the writings and drawings thereon, I trust that Frank O. Miller will inscribe in permanent form the story of his supreme moment, when patriotism overcame sentiment, and duty elbowed his sense of drama into the background.

The loyalty of Frank Oscar Miller transcends all other stories of its kind, for it was loyalty shown long after the last shot was fired and when war was a subject abhorrent equally to the tax-payer and the magazine editor, and when you might expect a man of romantic character to take a lenient view of his responsibilities to that state in which it had pleased God to place him.

There was a time when Frank O. Miller was just plain Franz Oscar Müller. He had changed his name in the 'nineties, having acquired by marriage service and purchase the business of Sloane Miller, Limited. It was in deference to his father-in-law's wishes, who, having no son, desired the perpetuation of his name, that Franz O. became Frank O.

The company had prospered exceedingly. The Sloane Miller building, with its twelve floors and its gilded cupola is a monument to Millerian industry. The Miller demesne at Hampstead is a palace, and Mrs. Miller's emeralds, which are kept, according to all account, in a small safe between the twin beds in Mr. and Mrs. Miller's gorgeous bedroom, are worth a king's ransom.

Incidentally, many men who were in no ways interested in securing the liberty of distressed monarchs had attempted to prove that assertion. But Mr. Miller was a pretty handy man with a gun. His safe was electrically controlled, and after Pal Morris, Lew Jakobs, and "Flash" Joe had successively made their attempts, had failed, and had passed to their country homes, it was agreed in the circles whence they came that Mrs. Miller's emeralds were not perhaps worth trying for, Even "Snakie" Smith, Unelected President of the Guild, and swellest and cleverest of all the mobsmen, turned down the proposition without looking at it, though he might as well have tried because he was caught a few weeks later in compromising circumstances (and a bank vault) and went out of town. This was in the year of grace 1909, and the emeralds have increased in value and size and general magnificence, and the Sloane Miller building has risen, and Mr. Miller himself has grown stouter since then, and the first Mrs. Miller has died and has been succeeded by the second Mrs. Miller (born Stohwasser).

Miller was always British in sentiment, and genuinely so. No suspicion ever attached to him. He subscribed heavily for War stock, gave largely to all the war charities, and if he had had one son he would have sent him with the first divisions to fight for freedom. Unhappily, he was childless.

He was sitting in his library one night in the early part of this year, when Jackie Strauss came in, dropped his hat on the floor, hunched himself into the corner of a settee, and swore thickly through his cigar. Mr. Miller looked over his spectacles at his old friend.

"What's wrong, Jackie?" he asked.

Jackie growled something, and a slow smile spread over the placid face of the head of the Sloane Miller Corporation, for that day he had pulled off a business deal, beating his competitors to the wire, and the chief of his competitors was the Strauss Machinery Trust, Limited. But it was evidently not the successful rivalry of his friend which disturbed Mr. Strauss.

"We've won the war, haven't we?" he demanded, fiercely, and he was evidently speaking under the stress of a strong emotion. "We've got Germany like that." he put his big thumb down suggestively. "Ain't that so? Well, why don't we leave 'em alone? See here, Franz. I'm British. To me there isn't a country like this in the world—though they tried to intern me. The only time I have been in Germany in the last twenty years I was treated like a criminal. But you've got to admit, Franz, he's the Big Man. He may have made this war or he may not. But he did make Germany big."

"We've won the war, haven't we?" he demanded, fiercely.

Mr. Miller took off his glasses, folded them slowly, and put them in his waistcoat pocket. He looked at his companion dubiously and thoughtfully, and rubbed his nose with the knuckle of his forefinger, a sure sign of his perturbation. There was no need to ask who "he" was. He knew instinctively, and there was a little echo of approval in the secret deeps of his mind.

"Don't talk like that in front of Bertha," he said, after a while. "Bertha is—" he hesitated.

Loyalty to his wife prevented his completing the sentence.

"Well, she's never been wholly with us, Jackie, as you well know."

Mr. Strauss nodded.

"I won't say that you're not right," Mr. Miller went on. "I don't like to see a man kicked when he's down, but I'm British first, Jackie."

"Ain't I?" demanded Jackie, truculently, his grey-shot moustache bristling; "but I've got something here," he pounded his spotted waistcoat with his fists, "right down inside me that makes me go just cold and sick when I hear these fools, who never had an original thought in their lives, talking about trying him and hanging him! I'm a Brandenburger, Franz. My relations for hundreds of years have been Brandenburgers. It's in my blood and soul, this feeling for—for him. I don't care if he's guilty as hell. I don't care if we suck Germany dry, if we chuck her fleet on the muck-heap—I'm for him!"

Mr. Miller shifted uneasily. He had his own feelings, for his ancestry went back to the Mark, and the best-known of his ancestors had been body-servant to the Great Elector himself.

"Don't say anything in front of Bertha about this," he repeated, mildly.

"Why not? And don't say anything about what?" asked a voice behind him, and he turned to meet the cold eye of Bertha Miller (née Stohwasser), who never called herself anything but Müller.

She was a good-looking woman in the early forties, dark, swarthy, cold of eye and manner, and now she looked from`her husband to his guest.

"Jackie's been talking politics," said Mr. Miller, feebly.

"I heard. Who is the 'he' you're speaking about?" she asked.

"Oh, never mind," said Mr. Strauss, loyally. "I hear you got that contract to-day, Franz—" "You were talking about the Emperor," said Mrs. Miller, not to be put off, "and I agree with you, Jackie. It's an abominable shame, the way people are talking. There isn't a worse-represented man in the world."

"Let's have some coffee,"? said Mr. Miller, hastily; "and for Heaven's sake, Bertha, get off that subject."

"You know it," she accused, "but you haven't the spirit of Jack Strauss. I can't understand how you can stand by and hear these people abuse him. I told that wretched woman, Sanderson, to-day just what I thought of her when she said they ought to hang him."

"Oh, lord," said Mr. Miller, in dismay, "why don't you keep your mouth shut? I'm a businessman, and I can't afford to have my business ruined, and ruined it will be if your views get about. People will say they are mine."

"Pah!" said the wife of his bosom, contemptuously, and addressed herself to Mr. Strauss. "It breaks my heart every time I think of it," she said, passionately; "I can hardly let my mind dwell on it. Think of it, Jackie! He who has had all the kings of Europe at his feet, who had only to lift his hand to have the world shake, who put Germany high amongst the nations, and is now an exile in a little Dutch village, lonely—"—her voice choked.

Mr. Miller, looking from her to his friend, saw a light in the eye of Jackie which he had not seen before, a suppressed eagerness which was more eloquent than speech—saw him lean forward and lay his hand on Mrs. Miller's arm.

"But is he?" he asked, softly.

"Is he what?" she answered, her handkerchief half-way to her eyes.

"Is he at Amerongen?"

She dropped her hands on her lap and stared at him.

"What do you mean?"

"I wasn't going to tell you," said Strauss, speaking quickly "but I guess it's got to come out, and I know I can trust you both. Who has seen the Kaiser at Amerongen? Nobody! The reporters have stood at the gates and have seen somebody in a grey cloak. But who has seen his face? A few villagers who have never seen the Emperor in their lives, and they only know it's him because they are told. Who, who has seen the Emperor in the life, has seen him at Amerongen? Nobody! We only know he's there because we are told he's there."

"I wasn't going to tell you," said Strauss, "but I guess it's got to come out.

"What do you mean?" asked Mrs. Miller again, her breath coming faster.

Strauss drew his chair nearer to her and lowered his voice.

"I'll tell you," he said. "One of my cashiers, a man named Tells, embezzled nearly a thousand pounds from me. That was five years ago. He was arrested and sent to penal servitude for five years. He was a married man, and I did all I could for him, and I told him when he came out of prison he was to come and see me. He turned up last week—" He paused impressively.

"Well?" said Mr. Miller, not the least interested of the two.

"I don't think he'll go straight. He's got into pretty bad company," Strauss went on; "in fact, he is already a member of a gang working under 'Snakie' Smith. You have heard of him! He's the biggest thing in the criminal world, and he came out of prison a week before Tells. Now, these criminals," he went on, speaking slowly and with emphasis, "have an intelligence organization of their own. There is hardly a Government secret that they're not up to, and lately some of them have been approached to shepherd a mysterious man who is coming from the Continent and is on his way to America."

Mr. Miller rose quickly.

"Pshaw!" he said. "Impossible! Why should they engage those kind of fellows to look after—? Bah! It's ridiculous!"

He was agitated, and showed it.

Mrs. Miller sat with her bright eyes fixed upon Strauss. She was in a rosy dream of glory, in that glow of exaltation which the novice before the altar, or the Eastern bride meeting her lover for the first time face to face, might experience.

"Go on," she whispered.

"Who could better look after him than these men who spend their lives dodging the police?" said Mr. Strauss, speaking rapidly, "and I tell you that the Emperor is not in Holland. Tells hinted at it."

"Rubbish!" said Miller, his voice quavering. "Would they put him at the mercy of a bunch of crooks? Why, at any moment any one of them might go to the police!"

"And be dead in twenty-four hours," said Mr. Strauss grimly; "you know their code, that class of person. I have looked up Smith's record. He is the very man who would undertake this work; a daring, resourceful man, with a good manner. He has been in every big crime that has been committed in this city since he was a boy of fifteen."

Mrs. Miller sighed, the long happy sigh of a dreamer.

"He may come here—to London.... Wonderful! Wonderful!"

"Dam' stupid!" snapped Miller. "I tell you I'm not in this, Strauss. I am real genuine British. They've treated me decently. The laws of this country are my laws, the enemies of this country are my enemies."

His wife turned in a fury.

"And you can say that, you can say that!" she hissed, "you a Brandenburger at heart! Don't you feel—doesn't your heart leap at the very thought of it?"

"No," said Mr. Miller, truthfully.

This was the guilty secret which he carried to his office, which walked at his elbow in the crowded street, which sat at the opposite side of his desk in his suite on the eighth floor of the Sloane Miller building. He saw Jackie Strauss the next day and purposely avoided him. He gave up eating at his favourite restaurant in Piccadilly and patronized the less fashionable Soho, where he knew Jackie, with his luxurious taste, would not venture.

Mrs. Miller saw Jackie frequently. She had consultations with him, and they met at lunches and at teas. Once at dinner in the family mansion, when the servants had been dismissed, she started in to tell her husband.

"Jackie thinks—" she began, and Franz Miller dropped his knife and fork with a crash.

"I don't want to know what Jackie thinks," he said, sternly; "now, get that stuff out of your mind, Bertha. If you insist upon remaining a German, remember that a German woman's first duty is obedience to her husband."

"But I want to tell you—"

"I don't want to know," roared Mr. Miller, purple of face, and emphasizing his words with thunderous smacks on the table. "I tell you I don't want to know. You're mad, Bertha, stark, staring, raving mad."

"He's not at Amerongen," blurted his wife, triumphantly.

"He may be with the devil for all I care," roared Miller. "Perhaps you are right, perhaps that crazy story is true, but I tell you I don't want to know, and if you don't stop talking—I'll— I'll—"

He looked so ferocious, and his hand clutched the plate so convulsively, that his wife wilted. He apologized for his anger after dinner, and she received his apology meekly.

The Millers made a point of retiring for the night at 11.30, and Franz was smoking his last cigar and reading for the last time the closing prices, when the butler came into the room.

"There's a man who wishes to see you, sir."

Mr. Miller had a sinking sensation at the pit of his stomach.

"Er—a man," he stammered.

He did not look at his wife, for he could almost feel the emanation of her radiant mind.

"Rather a tough-looking fellow, sir. He wants to see you privately."

Miller hesitated.

"Show him in here," he said.

"Perhaps—" whispered a voice at his elbow.

"Be silent, woman!" he thundered.

It was a relief to hear the sound of his own harsh, aggressive voice, and he found courage in his own violence.

The man who followed the butler was certainly not the man Mr. Miller dreaded to see. He was a short, bull-necked fellow, with keen, intelligent eyes, and a straight line of mouth. He waited till the butler had retired.

"I've got a message for you," he said, gruffly. "I dare say you've seen me before."

"I don't know—who are you?" asked Mr. Miller, suspiciously.

The man looked round to see that the door was closed.

"I am 'Snakie' Smith," he said.

"Yes, yes," broke in Mrs. Miller, impetuously; "have you a message?"

The man searched his pockets, produced a large white envelope and handed it to the reluctant Mr. Miller.

"Say," he said, confidentially, "I'm not in this. You don't know me. See? If anybody asks you whether 'Snakie' Smith has been, you have never heard of me!"

"No, of course not," said the woman, eagerly.

"Will you be quiet, Bertha?" demanded Mr. Miller, angrily. "Why should I compromise myself? What is this letter about?"

He did not open it, he dared not open it, and the messenger, noting his agitation, grinned.

"So long," he said, with a familiar nod of his head and, swinging round, stepped quickly into the hall, where the butler was awaiting him, and they heard the thud of the street door close behind him.

Mr. Miller turned the letter over and over. It was addressed to him in a large, sprawling, and unmistakably German hand.

"Open it, Franz," said his wife, in an agony of suspense.

Mr. Miller took a long breath and opened the envelope. The sheet which he extracted was of heavy paper, and on the top left-hand corner was a double-eagle, embossed in black. He adjusted his glasses with trembling fingers and read:

"At 11.30 to-night there will arrive one who has no home but the hearts of his people. Give him your hospitality for three nights before he passes on."

He read it three times and handed the letter to his wife. She stood rapt, transfigured, her eyes fixed upon the page.

"It's true," she whispered. "My God! It's true! How wonderful!"

Miller stood, a helpless, ludicrous figure, his mouth agape, his pale blue eyes wandering about the room, then—

"I've got to do it!" he said, hoarsely, "I've got to do it!"

He turned his pale face to his wife.

"Send the servants to bed." he said: "tell them we have a guest. He must have the best mom in the house. Will you—"

"I'll see to it. I'll see to it." she said, in a choked voice, and flew from the room.

He sat heavily down in a low chair, his head between his hands, bewildered, crushed. It seemed that the whole direction of his orderly life had been taken from his hands, He was in the grip of a force and a power stronger, more infallible than reason. This was Fate, Kismet, the Inevitability which was more tremendous than his will could harness. It crept over him, this new spirit of servitude, this atavistic impulse to obey. The blood of dead generations of Müllers who had buckled on their swords and tramped to the red West as the word of their sovereign lord sung through his veins, but to him the song was a dirge.

It was a quarter to twelve when the sound of a motor-car coming up the drive brought him to his feet. The car stopped before the house. There was a little interval and then a bell tinkled. He himself went to the hall and threw open the door.

The car was moving on as he did so, but a man was standing in the entrance, a medium-sized man, covered from shoulder to heel in a long black cloak, a soft felt hat of the same hue was pulled over his eyes, and in one hand he carried a battered portmanteau.

Mr. Miller mumbled something and bowed from his hip downward. He had never bowed like that before, but he knew that he must do so. The stranger stepped into the hall without a word and the door was closed and bolted behind him.

Mrs. Miller was in the open doorway of the library. She stumbled forward, caught the stranger's hand and, bending, kissed it.

"This is the way," she said, huskily, and went before him, Mr. Miller bringing up the rear.

She stumbled forward, caught the stranger's hand and, bending, kissed it.

The stranger stripped his cloak with his right hand—they noticed that he kept his left in his pocket—and with the same motion took off his hat. Tears blinded the woman. She could only see the dim outlines of a well-beloved face. Mr. Miller, though his pulse was beating a tattoo, noted the sallowness, the trim up-turned moustache, less exaggerated than he had expected, the tired eyes, the firm chin, the hair brushed straight back from the forehead.

"Is—would you like something to take?" he asked, shakily; "would your Majesty—"

The stranger raised his hand.

"You will please not use that word," he said, and his voice was gentle and sad. "I fear I am embarrassing you."

"No, no, certainly not," gasped Mr. Miller; "would you like some wine?"

The stranger shook his head.

"I am very tired," he said; "perhaps you would show me to my room. I am afraid I have not a servant."

His smile was very sweet. As he stooped to pick up the bag Mrs. Miller made a movement to forestall him.

"No, no," he said, gently, "I can manage myself. I must not be a greater trouble to you than I can help."

"It is no trouble, oh, I assure you it is no trouble," she cried. "If Exzellenz—"

"You must give me no title—please," he said, and he inclined his head toward the door.

She led the way up the stairs, though her knees were shaking under her, and again Mr. Miller brought up the rear.

"I could ask no better than this," said the man. He had been wearing under his cloak a stained grey uniform that fitted him like a glove. It was plain, without any ornament or decoration, but it was unmistakable.

"I came on a tramp steamer," he said; "it was rather—uncomfortable."

He dismissed them with a bow, and with no further word, and they went down together and sat for two hours facing one another, speechless.

At 2.30 Mr. Miller rose.

"I am going to bed," he said, heavily; "you have arranged—"

She nodded.

"I will see to his breakfast myself; nobody is to go into the room. I have told Parker and he will tell the servants that it is a friend who is ill."

"So?" said Mr. Miller, and mounted to bed, but not to sleep.

He went to his office the next morning, a criminal in mind and, if truth be told, in appearance. He lunched at a restaurant even more remote than any he had yet patronized. Somehow he dreaded returning to his secret, and, dismissing his car, he made a leisurely way homeward by motor bus.

Mrs. Miller was a very subdued, silent woman, but the fit of exaltation was still on her. She walked and moved as one who had seen a vision; was laconic but humble. When she spoke of the stranger her voice dropped to a pitch of reverence.

"I have only seen him tor a little while," she said; "I took his lunch and breakfast to him. To-night when the servants are in bed he wishes to take a stroll in the grounds. Will you—will you accompany him?"

"No," said Mr. Miller, shortly. He gulped. "No," he repeated. Then the grip of the old service fastened about his neck. "Yes, I will," he said.

It was a melancholy exercise, for neither spoke. The stranger walked a little in advance, his head bowed, his mind evidently occupied. As for Mr. Miller, he was torn between his old devotion and his new allegiance.

"I'm British!" he kept muttering to himself, as though it were some magic incantation which, repeated often enough, would restore his equilibrium.

The second day was a repetition of the first, but at nine o'clock came a diversion. Another stranger called, a clean-shaven, alert-looking man, who craved a private interview, and was ushered into the library, Mr. Miller quaking with apprehension.

"Sorry to bother you at this`hour of the night, Mr. Miller," said the stranger, briskly. "My name is Floyd. I am from Scotland Yard."

Franz did not faint. He stretched out an unsteady hand and caught the back of a chair for support.

"Oh, yes," he said, faintly; "a detective?"

"That's it, sir," said the brisk stranger. "It has been reported to me that an old friend of mine was seen giving your house a look-over the other day."

"The other day?" repeated Mr. Miller, mechanically.

"Four or five days ago," said the detective, and Mr. Miller breathed more freely. "He's a well-known thief named Smith—'Snakie' Smith: you may have heard of him."

"Oh, yes," said Mr. Miller; "Smith—er-did come to the house at—er—my invitation."

"At your invitation?"

"Yes," said the other. "The fact is, Mr. Floyd, I am—er—trying to reform him, getting him to go straight."

Floyd smiled indulgently as a father might smile at the fancies of her child.

"Reforming him, eh? Well, you've got some job! He's a bad boy, Mr. Miller. He's the man who got away with Mabel Joyce's tiara, the actress, you know. He was in the same company."

"I've heard about it," said the desperate Mr. Miller, "but I really think he is reforming now."

"You'll find it an expensive process," said Floyd, grimly.

He took his leave, but the relief at his departure was nothing like the relief that Mr. Miller felt that the police had noted the arrival of "Snake" Smith but had not observed The Man. He must be warned. If the police were watching "Snake," sooner or later they would hit upon their greatest discovery.

But he had no opportunity of warning. He could only tell his wife, and somehow he had got out of the habit of discussing things with his wife and had hardly spoken to her since the stranger had arrived. Yet he managed to convey something of his fears to her. He came back earlier the next day, and if she had been exalted before she was now so beyond recognition. She hardly waited for the door to close on him before she told her news.

"He is leaving to-night, Franz," she whispered. "A car will call for him at eleven. He is going West... on to America. He has friends there. Oh, and Franz, don't think that everything is lost. He has loyal friends. They are working for him, Franz, and he will come to his own. He will wrest from their hands everything they have stolen from him. In a few years, Franz, he will be great again, and you and I—"

"Great again?" said Mr. Miller, dully; "great! That is war!"

She babbled more news, but he did not hear it. All that he realized was war and what it meant, the wrecked lives, the maimed bodies, the sufferings, and a coming again of that hideous nightmare—war!

He did not speak through dinner. He sat hunched up in his chair while she talked in low, fierce tones, and the hands of the clock went round. Why, it was a crime! It was a sin, the most damnable sin that had ever been committed, and he was a participant in the villainy! There would be more war, more dead, more poor maimed, blind souls groping and groaning through the world!

He leapt up with a strangled cry and stumbled across the table to the telephone. His wife stared at him.

"What are you doing?"

He did not reply to her; his trembling hands turned the pages of the Telephone Directory, and presently he called for a number.

"What are you doing?" she asked again.

"Is that Scotland Yard?" he asked. "It is Mr. Miller speaking, of Sloane Miller, Limited. Yes, I am speaking from my house. I have got a man here you want."

"Is that Scotland Yard?" he asked. "I have got a man here you want."

She leapt up at him like a tigress and knocked the telephone from his hand.

"You sssha'n't, you sha'n't!" she screamed. "You traitor! You traitor! I'm going to warn him!"

She took two steps, but he was after her, had swung her round and had thrown her sprawling on to the couch.

"You stay here," he said, breathlessly. "You stay with me here. Don't you move!"

"I'll scream!" she whimpered. "You traitor! Your name will be execrated—"

She moved on, but he stood between her and the door to the hall.

He looked at the clock on the mantelpiece. It showed ten minutes to eleven. Then there came to his strained ears the "Chuff! Chuff!" of two motor bicycles.

His wife was as white as death. She sat glaring at him till he almost collapsed under the strain of her fanatical hate. Then the door opened, and it was Floyd who came in.

Mr. Miller tried to speak but could not. He raised his hand to his trembling lips to steady them.

"There's a man you want," he said, and got no farther, for at that moment the second door to the room opened and the stranger came in.

He was carrying his bag, his cloak was on his shoulders, and at the sight of Floyd he stood stock still.

"I want you, 'Snakie,'" said Floyd, and his automatic pistol covered the other.

"Well, well, well," said the Kaiser, "if it isn't Floyd!"

Both his hands were in the air now as he walked calmly toward them. He gazed benevolently from the shaking Mr. Miller to his speechless wife.

"And which of you unpatriotic devils put your Kaiser away?" he asked, in elegant English.

Mr. Floyd saw a bulge in the stranger's pocket, and unceremoniously put in his hand and drew forth that which restored Mrs. Miller to speech. It was a large handful of priceless emeralds.

"You nearly got away with it, too," said Floyd, admiringly. "Well, you are certainly the boy!"

The Kaiser smiled pleasantly.

"Have you got a friend outside?" he asked. Floyd nodded.

"I'm sorry," said the man. "Do you mind if I take my moustache off?—it tickles. I am afraid you owe me an apology, Mr. Miller," he said; "that you should imagine the bull-necked tough I sent to you was me hurts my pride."

There was a sound of motor wheels.

"Stocky Jones and Tells, I suppose?" suggested Mr. Floyd, with an inquiring jerk of his head to the sound; "they've been working with you. That car will come in handy." he added. "Pick up your bag, 'Snakie,' you don't suppose I'm going to valet you, do you?"

They went out together, leaving a very silent couple.

It was Mr. Miller who spoke first.

"Bertha," he said, clearing his voice, "You didn't kiss his hand before he went!"

He felt he was entitled to that one.

The Caretaker in Charge

A Wise Y. Symon Story

A police reporter has many interests and many friends, most of them queer. He spends his life in an atmosphere the principal ingredient of which is suspicion. Wise Y. Symon was a great police reporter, a veritable Napoleon of police reporters, and his greatness was due in no small degree to the fact that he preserved his faith in human nature. And, I have observed, that the title to greatness is often based upon the proper admixture of conflicting virtues.

There was a girl who used to go to work in the city office of a firm of lawyers in Waldorf House who interested Wise Symon immensely. He got to know her four years before this story opens, at a time when she was known to every reporter in town, and her portrait, large or small as the exigencies of space dictated, was to be found in almost every morning or evening journal.

The disappearance of her father, Harrigay Ford, was a nine days' wonder, and there came a time when newspapers no longer interviewed his daughter or printed the statements of trans-Atlantic stewards who had recognised him as the mysterious passenger who took his meals in his cabin.

After all. a wealthy man has the right to appear and disappear as he wishes. The story died when his banker, the patriarchal Mr. Borthwick. intervened. Harrigay Ford had gone abroad and had written a hasty note on the letter-heading of the S.S. Creptic saying that he expected to be absent from England for some years, and directing Mr. Borthwick to pay to the daughter of the said Harrigay Ford the sum of £100 per annum, payable quarterly.

It was a pretty mean allowance for a millionaire to make to his motherless child, and his only excuse could have been that he hardly knew he had a daughter. For Mr. Ford was a pillar of alcoholic fire by night and a dopey cloud by day.

Eileen Ford did not grieve for her parent. She lost nothing by his disappearance. She lived in her father's big house and sent the bills to his banker, and the bills were paid. But £100 a year was hardly the income that went with the style in which she lived, and after the Ford Case had disappeared from the scare headings, she went to a school of stenography, learnt the relative positions of Q.W.E.R.T.Y.U.I.O. and P. on the keyboard of a typewriter, and raised her annual income by another £100 in the prim offices of Atkins and Walters, solicitors.

Symon's friendship with the girl survived his newspaper interest in her fortune, and probably that is why the strange behaviour of Mr. Hopper attracted more than its share of his attention, and why the sequel to that attention brought the scoop of scoops to the humming presses of the Telephone Herald.

To say that the office or even the presses of the Telephone Herald hummed is, of course, a picturesque inexactitude. Newspaper offices do not hum. They bang and they squeak and they click-clack-click but they do not hum. Glass doors swing recklessly, wet men buttoned to their chins dash madly in, throwing off their moist coats and saying unprintable things about Great Public Favourites who deliver addresses on 'Labour' at inaccessible places in the most impossible weather.

The carriers in pneumatic tubes whine and plop! The linotypes which, by special arrangement, are invariably sited over the reporters' room, rumble and clack mysteriously, and ever and anon a plaintive voice cries 'Boy!' A small and grimy democrat wipes his jammy mouth with the back of his hand and hurries breathlessly to collect the literature. This literature is written in grey pencil and tastefully decorated with blue strokes by a super-editor.

At a little before midnight one snowy evening Wise Y. Symon drifted into the night editor's presence and lay down on his desk. The wise man invariably lay down on anything he couldn't rest his foot upon. His modus operandi was to get to the end of the desk and, doubling himself up like a foot rule, deposit the upper portion of his body east and west so to speak, resting his chin upon his hands.

The night editor pushed back his chair with a sigh, dropped his shell- rimmed spectacles to the end of his nose, and eyed Wise Symon sadly.

'Where's that story?' he asked at random.

'What story?' demanded Symon.

The night editor sniffed.

'You don't know anything about it, O,' accused Mr. Symon (the night editor's name was Oliver, and he was referred to either as 'O' or 'The Olive.')

'Well, what are you doing here, anyway?' complained Mr. Oliver fretfully. 'There's a newspaper got to go to bed. Have you never heard that such things happen?'

'Could I know anything of the underworld and not know that?' asked Symon reproachfully. 'No, my O, I have not come here to gloat over you. I do not climb into gay clothing for the joy of paying tantalising calls on the slaves of diurnalism. I have a reason for this mysterious visit.'

Wise Symon was in evening dress, and he was beautiful to behold, from the crest of his well-brushed head to the base line of his twinkling shoes.

'I noticed that,' said the patient Oliver, swinging round in his chair and lighting his pipe. 'You can hire these things, I understand—but you have to buy the shirt. Where have you been dining, Y, and on whom?'

Mr. Symon produced with much ostentation a gold case and extracted a large Turkish cigarette.

'I have been dining with a great bank official,' he said carefully, 'a man of infinite charm and sagacity. I have a further appointment with him at one o'clock, at which hour I proceed to his costly and palatial flat where, surrounded by every evidence of refinement and luxury, I shall endeavour to extract the body of a story, the slippery tail of which is already within my hand.'

'Loud cheers!' said the night editor wearily. 'Now, having delivered the speech of the evening, if you will kindly take your elbows out of my ink-pot, I will resume my little job of work refreshed '

'And invigorated,' finished Y. Symon, the star amongst police reporters, 'by the clarity and logic— Here's the old man. O.'

The 'old man' was the managing editor of the Telephone Herald, and at that moment he wore the facial expression peculiar to managing editors at midnight—an expression which may be likened to that of a man who has an engagement with the public executioner and is anxious to commit just another tiny little murder before he dies. He saw Symon, who belonged to the charmed circle which gathers at the daily editorial conference when even matters of policy are discussed, and started back with an affectation of faintness at the sight of Mr. Symon's society kit.

'Hello, Symon—why this disguise?'

'I have been dining with a gentleman,' said Mr. Symon magnificently. 'We had real wine and real cigars.'

'Police reporters should keep their places,' said the editor, 'you'll get your head turned. Who was the swell crook?'

'William Haliburton Hopper,' said Y solemnly.

'Hopper?' The editor frowned. 'He's not on my wine list. I don't even remember that he is in the class. What did he make, aeroplane or margarine?'

'William is no vulgar profiteer.'

Wise Symon sat on the edge of the nearest desk which was unoccupied, and there was a puzzled look in his eyes.

'You can guess that I am not wasting time on any ordinary millionaire,' he said. 'If William had no other recommendation than a taste for bad wine and toothpicks, I should have let him run loose. It's only lately that William has dawned upon the world of fashion. I met him drinking solitary in the grill-room of Petroni's about a week ago. It may have been his rough neck, or the butt of the gun I saw sticking out of his hip pocket, or the saucy talk he was handing to the waiter, but one of these things attracted me. So I palled up with him and we talked a while. He wanted to see life; he had bags of money and an infinite capacity for sweet champagne. Ugh! Well, it was interesting. He has the mentality of a goat, and a vocabulary that's strictly limited to about a hundred nouns and six adjectives.'

'How did he make his money?'

'He said he inherited it from his uncle. But he doesn't look like the kind of man who ever had an uncle. I shadowed him but he slipped me. Tonight we met by appointment—and I saw him home.'

He paused.

'He is the caretaker of Borthwick's Bank.'

'That sounds good for old man Borthwick,' said the editor after a moment's silence. 'Does the caretaker sleep on the premises?'

Wise Symon nodded.

'Yes and no. He rents a flat near the bank in addition. That is where I am meeting him.'

'And he spends his spare time up West loading himself up with champagne?' said Hammond. 'H'm! Well, old Borthwick must know this. His bank has always been a shaky affair, and a hint of this sort of thing might smash him. He nearly went broke four years ago. Are you seeing the caretaker again?'

'Yes. But he told me that he had some business to do before he saw me again, and naturally that piqued my curiosity. I followed him and saw him turn into the side entrance of the bank. Then I remembered him. I had seen him sweeping the steps—I pass the premises every day.'

The editor looked at his watch.

'I was going home, but I think I'll wait for you. When will you be back?'

'Not later than by three,' said Wise Symon. 'It looks a good kind of story to me, and I'd like to get the full facts in type before the police rope him in.'

Mr. Hammond nodded.

'It's a good story, and the public like this kind of case—the working man by day and the millionaire by night stuff. But you'll have to break the news to Borthwick before the police start moving/

It was a quarter to three when Wise Symon came into the managing editor's office.

'It's a rum story.' he said, dropping his soaking hat on the floor. 'Hopper told me nothing except that he could wrestle with the best wrestler in the world, and he could drink three times more than any other man in the world—neither of which items of information was particularly helpful/

He stopped and the editor, stretching back in his chair, looked up at him.

'Out with it—you discovered something you did not expect to discover?'

Wise Symon shook his head.

'No, sir. I'm disappointed. I hoped to make a discovery—and didn't.'

'We're both thinking the same thing, I expect.' said Hammond quietly. 'What have you got on your mind, Symon?'

'I'll tell you what I've got on what passes for my mind,' said Wise Symon, after a little hesitation. 'I associate this disgusting prosperity of Hopper with the disappearance of Harrigay Ford.'

'I thought you were going to say that.' The editor shook his head. 'It's a long time since Ford went, three or four years, and frankly I think your suggestion is fantastic, although I expected it. Did the man say anything which gave you the impression that he knew anything about Ford's disappearance?'

'Nothing,' said Wise Symon.

'What's your theory?'

'Ford was a drunkard and a dope fiend,' said Symon. 'Such men, as we know, are happiest in the most sordid and miserable surroundings, however cultured might have been their upbringing. I suggest that when four years ago Harrigay Ford disappeared he did not leave London. Yes, I know what you are going to say about the letter written on the steamship notepaper, but you or I could have done exactly the same thing. One could have boarded the steamer, written the note, posted it, and have never left the country. My theory is that Harrigay Ford is to be found in some low haunt in this city, that Mr. Hopper is his guardian and treasurer. I made inquiries yesterday, and I found that Hopper got his job at the bank on the recommendation of Ford.'

The editor scratched his chin.

'The thing to do, of course, is to see old Borthwick tomorrow. I happen to know that cheques signed by Ford come through fairly regularly and are cashed by Borthwick—Borthwick being his banker. The old man was telling me at the club only the other day how worried he was about the matter. At any rate, Borthwick would be able to tell you from where these cheques come. I think you will find they come from abroad. As to Ford being concealed in an opium den in this town—why. I'm sceptical! Those sort of things only happen in books.'

It was at half-past ten in the morning that Wise Symon turned into Borthwick's Bank. It was an unimposing little building, but had constituted the premises of some bank or other from time immemorial.

Borthwick's Bank was a private affair with very few clients, and its staff consisted of two elderly men who spent most of their time checking the fluctuations of the Stock Exchange, Mr. Borthwick being by all accounts somewhat overloaded with the collateral of his scanty clientèle.

One of the cashiers took Mr. Symon's card and disappeared with it through a door at the back of the premises. He returned to beckon Symon forward, and old Borthwick rose from behind the leather-covered table, where he spent most of his day reading through a large magnifying glass the press reports of foreign exchanges and transactions, and offered his big hand to the visitor.

He was a man who stood six feet in his stockings. He had one of those massive heads which Raphael loved to paint in such scenes as the apostles appeared. A snowy white beard reached down half way to his waist, a bluff, benevolent, shrewd old gentleman with a thunderous voice that was wholly in keeping with his hearty appearance, he seized Symon's hand in a grip that made that young gentleman wince.

'Sit down, sit down. Mr. Symon,' he bellowed. 'I remember you very well indeed. What have you come to bother me about?'

'I'm afraid I have no pleasant news for you,' smiled Symon. and told the story of the gay caretaker.

Mr. Borthwick listened with a troubled face.

'I am sorry he does that,' he said, when Symon had finished, 'it gets the bank a bad name.'

'But surely—' began the astonished Symon.

'Oh, it's his own money all right!' said Mr. Borthwick. 'He inherited a large sum of money from a brother who died in Australia. As a matter of fact, he has opened an account with us. I tried to persuade him to give up his work at the bank, but so far he has refused. Was he very drunk?' he asked.

'Pretty drunk,' said Symon, a little disappointed as all great artists are when their revelations fail to produce the sensation they anticipated. 'He told me that it was his uncle who had died.'

'Very possibly, very possibly,' said Mr. Borthwick. 'I know it was some sort of relation. And now as to the other matter, Mr. Symon?'

'I want to know if you have any news you can give me about Ford.'

'None, I am afraid,' the old man shook his head sorrowfully. 'What a terrible thing, Mr. Symon, what a terrible thing! Drink and drugs! Surely, that is a lesson which every young man can lay to heart!'

'When did you last hear from him, Mr. Borthwick?'

'About a week ago,' said the old man.

'Can you tell me in what country he can be found?' '

'I cannot tell you where he can be found at all,' replied Mr. Borthwick. 'I should be exceeding my instructions if I did, but I may say that he is in Australia.'

'Are you sure?' asked Symon, disconcerted for the second time.

'Absolutely sure,' said Mr. Borthwick.

He rose, walked to a safe and unlocked it. From a drawer he produced a cheque and handed it to the reporter. Wise Symon, who had a memory like a cash register, noted that its number was 1795, and that it was signed with Ford's signature—with which Symon was familiar. He handed it back.

'It arrived from Australia only two days ago,' said Mr. Borthwick, locking it back in the safe.

Wise Symon rose.

'Well, I think that's about all I have got to ask you,' he said, disguising as best he could his chagrin.

'You wouldn't like to buy a few Southern Pacifics while you are here.' said the jovial old man, 'one of my unfortunate clients has a parcel he would like to dispose of?'

'No, thank you, Mr. Borthwick,' said Wise Symon hurriedly, and he left the old banker chuckling.

His next call was upon the firm of lawyers which employed Ford's daughter, and he had no difficulty in persuading them to allow him to see her.

'No, Mr. Symon,' she replied, in answer to his question, 'I have not heard from my father. Have you?' she asked eagerly.

He shook his head.

'Do you get your allowance regularly?' he asked.

'Yes,' she said, 'such as it is.'

'Doesn't Mr. Borthwick ever give you a message from your father?'

'Never,' she said, a little sadly.

'How long has Mr. Borthwick been your father's banker?'

'Oh, for a very long time, longer than I can remember! They were old friends in the days before daddy was—' Her lips trembled.

'And after?'

'Well, after daddy wasn't very nice to Mr. Borthwick. He used to behave dreadfully to that poor old gentleman. Once he threatened to turn over his account to the National Bank, and that would have ruined Mr. Borthwick.'

'When was this?' asked Wise Symon.

'About a month before daddy went away—or it may not have been so long. I know Mr. Borthwick was very much distressed.'

He asked her a few other questions, but could get no information that was any more helpful than that which he already had. He met his editor at lunch and made a qualified admission of his failure.

'I didn't think Ford was in this town,' said Hammond, 'and the caretaker's legacy rather knocks the bottom out of your theories, my wise lad.'

'My theories are bottomless,' said Wise Symon. 'Anyway. I shan't meet William tonight as I promised. If he is only a vulgar legatee and not the interesting criminal I thought he was he has ceased to fascinate me.'

It so happened that a very commonplace elopement, in which there figured the daughter, the chauffeur, and the cashbox of a Society leader, kept the police reporter fairly busy. He turned in his 'copy' at eleven o'clock that night and had hardly stepped into the night editor's office when that worthy sprung at him, tore the 'copy' from his hands, and pushed him out again.

'Hustle, Y,' he said. 'Your caretaker, William Hopper—'

'What about him?' asked Y quickly.

'He was found shot dead tonight on a bench in the park. We've been looking for you all the evening.'

There were few details that Wise Symon could gather from the police. The man had obviously been murdered, since no weapon had been found near the spot where the body was discovered. A policeman on duty had heard the shot and had run in the direction, but did not meet the murderer.

The caretaker was in his ordinary working costume and was quite dead when he was found. A bunch of keys, a few shillings, and a plug of tobacco were his worldly possessions. Siddon, from Scotland Yard, was in charge of the case, and Siddon was particularly friendly to Wise Symon.

'You are sure nothing else was found on the body?' asked reporter.

'Here is everything,' said Siddon, pointing to the table in his office on which a miscellaneous collection of articles were displayed. 'There is no evidence to support your story that he was a very wealthy man unless you call this wealth.'

He picked up a crumpled scrap of paper and handed it to Symon. It was the half of a torn cheque, and on the back of it was scribbled the ciphers: £10,000.

Symon turned the cheque over and looked at the writing again, and his eyes were a blaze of triumph as he handed the paper back to the police officer.

'Jimmy Siddon,' said he, 'I am going to make your fortune: or, at any rate, I am going to make your name.'

'What do you mean?' asked Siddon. 'Do you know anything?'

'I know everything,' said Wise Symon. 'Let's go along and see old Borthwick. Bring that paper with you, and I think we shall be able to tell him a great deal more about his caretaker that he will just hate to hear.'

'Has the man been robbing him?' asked Siddon, as the taxi sped through the night towards Hampstead, where Mr. Borthwick had his severe but expensive rooms.

'You mean has he been robbing the bank? Honestly, I don't think he has. At any rate, if he had lived that is not the charge I should have made against him. Siddon, this story is mine; and you have got to keep the other journalistic ghouls at bay until I have spun it over a full page of the Telephone Herald.'

'You've got to make it a story yet,' said Siddon, who knew the requirements of the daily Press.

'It's made,' said Wise Symon.

Mr. Borthwick lived with two servants on the third floor of a big block of flats, but Mr. Borthwick was not at home. The housekeeper suggested that he might be found at his club.

'Let's try the bank,' said Wise Symon. 'He may be casting up his accounts.'

The bank was dark and silent.

'If you will condone the offence,' said Wise Symon, producing a bunch of keys from his pocket, 'we will do a little burglary.'

'Where did you get those keys?' demanded the detective chief.

'I smouched 'em when you weren't looking. They were part of Hopper's effects. Ah. here's the key!'

The door swung open noiselessly.

'Have you got an electric lamp?' whispered Symon.

'I don't like this,' growled the other, but produced the lamp.

They stepped into the dark passage and closed the door behind them. It ran parallel with the depth of the outer office. On the right was a stairway leading to the upper portion of the premises and presumably to Hopper's sleeping apartments. At the end was another door, which was only opened after almost every key on the bunch had been tried. They now found themselves in the outer office itself, facing Mr. Borthwick's private office.

Wise Symon touched his companion's arm and pointed. A thin line of light showed beneath the door. He stepped forward on tiptoe, turned the handle cautiously, and threw the door open.

Mr. Borthwick was sitting at the desk, his massive head on his hand, examining a small ledger. Behind him the steel door leading to the vaults of the bank was slightly ajar. At the first sound he leapt to his feet.

'Put that gun down. Borthwick!' said Wise Symon sharply. 'Put it down or I'll kill you a damn sight quicker than you killed Hopper.'

The old man was speechless. No longer benevolent was the light that shone in his eyes. He opened his mouth to speak, but there came an interruption. The door leading to the bank vault opened slowly and there cringed into the room a pallid, bearded figure, with shaking hands and bloodshot eyes, blinking from one to the other.

'Mr. Borthwick,' he piped pitifully, 'Mr. Borthwick, you're quite mistaken. Won't you let me explain? I did promise Hopper £10,000 if he let me loose. I wrote it on one of the cheques and passed it through the bars, but I wasn't going to betray you. Mr. Borthwick,' he sobbed, 'I swear to God I wasn't going to do you any harm.'

'Siddon,' said Wise Symon, 'this is Mr. Harrigay Ford, who, unless I am greatly mistaken, has been a prisoner in the vaults of this bank ever since he threatened to take his account elsewhere.'

'Old Borthwick was a gambler.' said Wise Symon to his chief in the early hours of the morning when the presses of the Telephone Herald were roaring with a note, as it seemed, of exultation at the ingenuity and enterprise of the staff. 'He has always been a speculator, and when Ford threatened to take his account away he knew he would be ruined. He got Ford when he was doped and put him in the vault. Don't you realise that all banks are built so that they make ideal prisons? The caretaker had to be in the secret—nobody else visited the vault. So the caretaker had to be paid. Ford was supplied with food, a chequebook, and a pen, and every time Borthwick's accounts wanted balancing he had to draw the cheque or suffer—the old man was as strong as a horse in spite of his age. I shouldn't think that Hopper had any communication with the prisoner, but apparently Ford tried to bribe him to secure his release, writing the sum he was willing to pay on the back of a cheque and slipping it into the caretaker's hand when the old man wasn't looking. Borthwick must have found this out. He was alarmed by my visit, but probably more alarmed by Hopper's attitude.'

'But how did you guess?'

'I didn't guess, I knew. The slip of paper found on Hopper's body inscribed £10,000 was written on cheque No. 1796, the very next to that which the old man told me had been drawn in Australia, apparently weeks before.'

'You're a real Wise Symon,' said the editor admiringly.

'Has anybody ever honestly doubted it?' said Mr. Symon.

The Magnificent Ensign Smith

There are many things about the late war (writes Dr. Halkeith-Sinclair, of Curzon Street) which I do not understand even in these days, when its secrets form the subject of daily official and unofficial communications, so that we learn of new and wonderful ships, marvellous new explosives, undreamt-of aeroplanes, and the like. Half-way through the narrative they told of the Magnificent Ensign Smith, I found myself wondering why the Government of the United States of America had been so grudging of the recognition it gave to his unparalleled devotion.

I came into this story in a most prosaic and commonplace fashion. At 9.30 one night in December I was in my surgery in Curzon Street, Mayfair, when I was rung up by the Hotel Savoy-Carlton. I was not in the best of moods, for two hours previously I had been called to a shooting case by the police, and no practitioner—and certainly no practitioner of my standing—cares to get mixed up in a criminal trial, involving as it does hours wasted in draughty court-houses. It was the manager of the Savoy-Carlton who called me.

"I wish you would come over, doctor, and see an American lady who arrived to-day by the Lapland."

"What is the matter with her?" I asked.

"I think she is pretty ill. I have had telegraphic instructions from some American officers in France to do everything possible for her, and I am rather scared of her appearance."

"All right, I'll come over," said I. I drove down to the Savoy-Carlton, which is one of the best hotels in London, and Colloni, the manager was waiting for me in the entrance hall.

"I'm sorry to bring you over, doctor, but I am afraid the lady is very ill. I wonder the American authorities allowed her to travel."

"Is she old or young?" I asked.

"She is old," he said, "and arrived here at five o'clock in a state of collapse. The American officers I spoke of had already booked a suite for her, and as Americans are amongst my best customers I do not want to offend them, otherwise I should have sent her straight to a hospital."

He took me up in the elevator, and there I saw my patient. There is a certain beauty about age, a quality which is called caducity, which means the beauty of decaying things. Her hair was white, her face was one of infinite sweetness, and I saw what I have so often seen in women's faces when they are approaching the great last test of their fortitude, an inspiring majesty. The nurse who was in attendance said she was the sweetest old lady she had ever attended, but "sweet" seems to me to be too mild and sugary a word. You could not call the Canadian Rockies sweet, or the tropical heavens, or the Grand Canyon, or the Valley of Chamonix—and She held something of the dignity of all these things.

I made a brief examination. There was no need to look far for the trouble. She had reached the end of all her physical resources, and it was little short of a miracle that she had been able to make the long journey from America.

She looked up into my face, which was as expressionless as I could make it, and smiled.

"You wonder I am alive," she said.

"Well, I wouldn't say that, Mrs. Smith," said I, pulling up a chair and summoning all my stock of reserve cheerfulness. "You are certainly a very daring lady to have taken this journey."

She smiled again.

"It was vanity," she said, and I laughed.

"Oh, yes, it was vanity."

Her voice was quite strong. She spoke without effort, and, so far as I could see, her respiration was normal. But it is absurd and profitless for a doctor to attempt to gauge by any scientific formula the values of will. Still more unsatisfactory must be any examination which science makes into the life-value of love.

"I am the mother of Ensign Smith," she said, and spoke with assurance, as though Ensign Smith were so well known a character that there was no need for further explanation.

"Oh, yes." said I.

She smiled again.

"Of course you're English, and you are not taking quite the same interest in our boys as we, and I cannot expect you to understand just how an American mother feels about her son who has died so gloriously—for Liberty."

Her eyes lit up with a light that rivalled the eyes of youth, a faint colour showed in the pale, wasted cheeks, and the thin hands which lay on the coverlet gripped the down-quilt.

"I don't think you ought to talk very much," said I; "it will excite you and keep you awake."

She shook her head slowly.

"Do you know what time the Continental train arrives in London?" she asked.

I explained to her that the Continental trains kept no particular time, especially the troop trains, and apparently it was the troop train she was expecting.

"They will be here," she said, with conviction, and was silent for a while, her head turned on her pillow, her eyes half closed.

Presently she raised them again.

"My son, Ensign Smith, won the Medal of Honour in the Argonne!"

"That's splendid!" I said, with enthusiasm, for I knew how jealously that medal is awarded in the American Army.

She nodded.

"Yes, it was splendid. But you don't know how splendid it was. You see Jimmy—" she hesitated. "Why, I'll tell you all about him, because he has so wonderfully redeemed his faults. Jimmy was a great trouble to me, dear lad. He went with the wrong set, and there was some—some unpleasantness in New York. He was always a delicate boy, and we spoilt him, I guess, and he got mixed up with evil men and women, and he—well, they used to come and tell me about him, and it well-nigh broke my heart. And even when he enlisted they said he was—drunk. But we worked hard for him, and the Governor, my brother-in-law, used his influence, and, well, Jimmy made good." She closed her eyes and smiled and repeated: "Yes, Jimmy made good. He was killed in the Argonne Forest. We didn't know what had happened, because the official news was that he had died, and I wrote to an officer who came from Palata, and he wrote back a beautiful letter about Jimmy, and said he had done splendidly and was going to be awarded the Medal of Honour."

She paused, and I hoped that she was not going to speak again, although I was more than interested. A doctor cannot afford to indulge in his emotions, but my heart went out to that pathetic figure with her beautiful pride.

But she was not, as I hoped, going to sleep. She was just thinking, and the smile did not leave her face.

"I knew he would not he awarded the Medal of Honour except for something very grand," she said; "and they couldn't tell me anything at Washington. Why, you'd think they would know everything at Washington, wouldn't you?"

I nodded.

"Well, they were just too busy, I guess. So one day the thought came to me that I would go to France, or perhaps to England, where I could get into touch with his comrades and his officers."

A light dawned on me.

"I see: so you told them you were coming and they offered to meet you here?"

She nodded.

"To-night?"

She nodded again.

"I have had a telegram from France. A deputation from the regiment is on its way. Isn't that wonderful? A deputation from the regiment to tell me about Jimmy!"

There came a tap at the door at that moment, and I walked over and answered it. It was the manager.

"There are three American officers, the gentlemen who hired the suite, and they want to see the lady. Can they, do you think?"

"I don't think it will make very much difference," said I, in a low voice.

"Is she so ill?"

I nodded.

"Perhaps I had better go down and see them, and explain."

When I turned my head I saw her eager eyes fixed on mine.

"They have come?" she asked.

"They have just come. Do you mind if I go down and see them?"

"Please don't keep them too long, doctor," she said. "I know just how sick I am, and I am only living to hear about Jimmy."

This I knew to be the truth.

I found the three officers waiting by the elevator, and the manager introduced me.

There was a tall, grey major and two younger officers, tired, brown-faced men, with the mud of France on their boots and that strange, set look which men wear who have been through the hell of the Argonne.

"You understand, Major," I said, "that Mrs. Smith is practically in extremis."

"I guessed that," said the Major—his name was Shore. "How long do you think she will live?"

"It is very difficult to tell," said I. "It may sound brutal to you, but she ought to be dead now. It is extraordinary that in her condition she can be either conscious or alive."

Major Shore exchanged glances with his two companions.

"Will you come up with us, doctor?" he said. "I'm pretty scared. I would like to have you around—in case."

I understood, and we went up in the elevator together in silence, and I did not speak again till I introduced them severally by their names—Major Shore, Captain Urqhuart, and Lieutenant van Roos.

I shall always remember the expectancy in her face, the fine comradeship in that shaking hand she extended to them, and shall never get from my mind the picture of those three solemn men sitting around the bed their faces contrasting with the live, joyous expression that she wore.

"It is very kind of you gentlemen to humour an old woman," she said. "Maybe you will have children of your own one of these days, and yon will know how I feel about Jimmy. And Jimmy had so many enemies who would never believe that he had that side to his character."

"Surely," said the Major, clearing his throat. "Why, jimmy was the gamest boy that ever served in the 34th, wasn't he, Urqhuart?"

"He was fine," said the captain, huskily. "I don't think I have ever had a better boy under me. He was in my company."

"And you lived with him?"

She was speaking half to herself, in a sort of rapt ecstasy. "Shared the same tent with him, perhaps?"

Urqhuart nodded.

"Saw him every day! Why, that almost deifies you boys in my eyes."

"He was with me!" It was young van Roos who spoke. "The day we went over!"

"Did he show any—" She hesitated to frame the words.

"He was the bravest of the brave," said van Roos, stoutly. "He was the first over. He went right ahead of the men. There was a big redoubt immediately in front of us, a regular nest of machine-guns, and our men were falling by the score, but Jimmy went on."

"Encouraging them, you see. Mrs. Smith," said Major Shore. "In moments like that example is everything. The bravest of soldiers wouldn't face that kind of fire if they saw their officer faltering."

"That's why Jimmy was so extraordinary," put in Urqhuart. "We never expected him to make that kind of show. The men rallied and went up after him, and we took the redoubt ten minutes later."

"Was he alive then?" she whispered.

"Yes, he was alive then," said Shore. "He wasn't killed till—later."

"And didn't the men think he was wonderful?" she asked.

"They surely did," said Urqhuart; "how could they think anything else? They called him the Magnificent Ensign Smith."

"Did they really, did they really?" she cried, clasping her hands. "I know, you wrote and told me!"

"There was nothing Jimmy wouldn't face." It was Shore who spoke now. They seemed to take it in turns to supplement the record of the boy's heroism. "Nothing worried him—shells, bombs, or machine-gun fire. He took it all laughing."

"And was he a good boy?" she asked, timidly. "I know boys get a little wild when they are out of the battle-line, and there are many temptations to young men. Did he drink?"

"Oh, no!" The three spoke together.

"No," said Major Shore, "I never met a better living fellow than Jimmy. He was just the cleanest lad you could wish to meet."

"He simply spent all his time studying military books," said van Roos. "We used to get rather tired of his studious ways. When the other fellows were going out to paint the town red you would always find Jimmy sitting tight in billets with a book on his knee."

"It made a man of him. It made a man of him!" she whispered.

"Why, it's difficult to believe that Jimmy was ever anything else," said Urqhuart, shaking his head; "he was just made for soldiering. You don't get many Jimmies, even in our Army."

She lay with closed eyes, and for five minutes nobody spoke.

"Tell me how he died," she said, after a while.

"It was at a little village called Piedmont," said Urqhuart. "It lay in a valley between two steep hills, and it was covered by a stream which flowed right across the line of advance. The village had been consolidated by the Germans, who held it in strength. Their batteries had got our positions registered to an inch, and the whole of the hillside was sprinkled with machine-guns. The Virginian regiment on our right had to work round the knoll to the east of the village, and we had to make a frontal attack straight into the gap. The engineers threw over a light bridge, but it was shot away by the German guns. Then the general called for volunteers to swim the stream under fire and establish a position on the north bank so that we could enfilade the German trenches which curved round the village to the west."

"Yes?"

"Well, Jimmy volunteered," said van Roos. "Yes, Jimmy volunteered to lead a platoon across. Of course, it was all done in a hurry, the arrangements were very hasty, and he had to take what men he could find in his sector. Our guns put down a barrage on the village, and Jimmy went over."

"Was he first across the stream?" she asked, hopefully.

"Absolutely first," said Shore. "I saw him through my glasses. I was back in an observation post and had a good view. He got into a ditch on the other side of the stream, and half-a-dozen men crawled in with him. It was certain death for the first to cross, even if they got to the other side."

"Jimmy had only six men," said Urqhuart.

"The next wave that tried to cross were shot to pieces, so Jimmy and his six went on and carried the first German machine-gun post at the point of the bayonet."

"Isn't that wonderful?" said the old woman in a hushed voice. "Don't you boys feel kind of proud of having served with him?"

They nodded.

"And was he—"

"He was killed right there in the German trench, killed instantaneously," said Shore.

"But his sacrifice was not in vain?" she asked.

"No," said Urqhuart. "Indeed no. He held the enemy at a critical point, and gave us just the opportunity we wanted."

"And they gave him the Medal of Honour?"

Major Shore put his hand in his pocket and brought out a flat leather care. He pressed a catch and it sprang open, revealing the simple emblem of valour. She took it reverently in both hands and raised it to her lips.

"Jimmy! Jimmy!" she whispered.

I have never seen anything more beautiful than the smile on her face when I took the medal from her dead hands.

Urqhuart was standing up by the other side of the bed.

"Is she dead?" he asked, in a low voice.

I nodded, and that big soldier went down on his knees by the side of the bed and sobbed as if his heart would break.

Presently be grew calmer and stumbled to his feet, wiping his face.

"Thank God, thank God!" he said. "Thank God that's over!"

He looked at the two men, from one strained face to the other.

"I don't know how you fellows feel, but I feel—horrible," he said, and they nodded.

I think with any encouragement they would have broken down, for their eyes were wet.

"It was my fault," Shore said; "I wanted to make it easy for her when I wrote about the Medal of Honour." He took the medal from my hands and fastened it to his own breast.

I stared at him.

"But didn't he get it?" I asked. "Surely a man who behaved—"

He shook his head, and though he smiled his lips were drooping.

"Ensign Smith," he said, "was shot for cowardice in the face of the enemy."

"I've been sitting here for four hours", said Commander Vanrhyn, of the U.S. Navy, and there was a note of disappointment in his deliberate speech, "and I've heard you boys telling what you consider is the most wonderful story of the war and I've said nothing. And what is more Bestwin has said nothing—which shows that we sailor-men, whether we are American or British, are possessed to a larger extent of what Napoleon called 'the greatest ornament of illustrious lives' than our comrades of the Army."

There was a howl of protest from the club smoke-room, for all present, save the American commander and Commander Sir George Bestwin, were of the land service.

"It is only modesty which prevents my telling you the story of the U904 which has never before been related—unless you've told it George?"

Sir George Bestwin shook his head gravely.

"It is not a story I am competent to tell," he said; "the honours are with you Vanrhyn."

"Well, I don't know," reflected Vanrhyn, "anyway it is a wonderful story."
I must begin this yarn at the beginning (said the Yankee sailor, yielding at last to the demand of the club) by telling you something about myself. No, Colonel, I am not forgetting Napoleon's dictum, but this explanation is necessary. I went into the Navy as a boy and served seven years, part of the time in the old coast-defence ship 'Miantonomoh'—but that's neither here nor there.

My naval career was uneventful and I left with the rank of Lieutenant on the death of my uncle. Uncle Harvey was the proprietor of one of the most prosperous newspapers in Chicago, which since I have no desire to advertise, I will call the Monitor-Post. By his death I became the sole proprietor of this proposition, and I only refer to the fact because it was in this new field of journalism that I first woke up to the fact that there was a mighty big world outside Chicago.

It was here that I was educated up to German mentality and learned that there was a place called Germany where men were not content with the realisation of modern ideals, but thought backward way into the dark ages, where the only law was the law of the sword, and the only right was the right of the stronger.

I am indebted to this day to my chief tutor, a cub reporter named Willie Mainz, who was a storehouse of information on militarism and for some extraordinary reason was proud of his ineffaceable right to be kicked by his masters as a normal citizen is of Pure Government.

I guess that Willie was never just as reliable on any other subject as he was on Germany and her future. He turned in stories which got us into no end of trouble. He had only to see a foreign looking woman registering as Mrs. Smith at an hotel to found a story of a Grand Ducal misalliance and the flight of the guilty couple to America, which got even the romances of old Dumas looking as mean as a meteorological report. He cost us too much money, and the staff wasn't big enough to allow us to send out four men to verify his facts, so we fired him, and I at least parted from him with regret.

Often after the European war started I have thought of all his predictions and how marvellously true they were. He foretold the invasion of Belgium, the U-boat campaign, the collapse of Russia—everything came true except the taking of Paris. I admit I had a genuine liking for the little fellow, and when the news reached Chicago that he had been killed at Verdun, I wrote his obituary with my own hand.

Now there was one prediction which I have thought about a great deal since America came into the war. I was discussing with Willie once, just before he left for Germany, this very question of convoys which we were talking about earlier in the evening. There was some discussion in the English Press in the early part of '15 as to whether merchantmen should or should not be convoyed. Emden and Karlsruhe and other light cruisers were playing the devil with English shipping at the time, and Willie had produced a map and shown me that it was impossible to protect shipping by any other means than sending with them an escort.

"Here," he said, pointing to the map—I won't tell you exactly where 'here' was—"is the only place where a patrol could protect an unarmed convoy, and even a U-boat could not get past because there is twenty miles of shallow water."

I tell you war strategy and German tactics were his consuming vices.

Well, the coincidence in this story—or one of them—lies in this fact, that early this year, having rejoined the Navy at the outbreak of war, I found myself in command of one of a flotilla of four destroyers, two of which were American and two British, patrolling this very area. That is why I say that Willie's words came back to me in the dark watches, and I often wished I could bring the young man back from the shambles of Verdun to repeat some of the points which I had forgotten.

Bestwin commanded one of the British destroyers and, as he will confirm, I had often discussed, in the light of Willie's information, the practicability of a U-boat evading the patrol and slipping through across the track of the U.S transports.

In April the Atlantic was thick with American troops bound for Europe and a pretty heavy strain was imposed on the patrols, when we received a wireless from the flagship that a tin-fish was loose in our neighbourhood and that it was one of the latest type. It had passed without sinking two small merchantmen in the English Channel, and that looked pretty ominous. Of course we got all the information which the English Intelligence Department could gather; the name of the commander was Scholtz, a well-known skipper, famous for his daring and resourcefulness, the boat's number was 904, and she had left Bremen on such and such a date.

Naturally, being a bit rattled by our responsibility, we wondered why the artist who had written her biography, so to speak, had not rounded off the job whilst he was admiring her classic lines and put a shell into her. For rattled we were, Bestwin and I. The patrol had been reduced to two, and away out there on the Atlantic were some 20,000 innocent doughboys full of pep and blissfully confident in the power of the Navy to hold back anything that sported a periscope.

I won't tell you the size and power of their escort. This was April, remember, men were badly needed in France, and we took a few risks what we don't take nowadays.

Our patrol covered the only deep water for a hundred miles and that wasn't too deep in places. It lay between two shoals and we had buoyed the four corners of the deep patch to save us the bother of continuously taking observations. Day and night we raced up and down, crossing and recrossing, or else lay with engines stopped, listening at the microphone for some sound of a submarine propeller.

I can testify that the night the U 904 got through we were on the qui vive. It was a calm, starlit night with scarcely any wind but a gentle breeze from the south. The sea was dead calm and I guess that if two lobsters had rubbed together we'd have heard them. And yet that U-boat got through. Patiently, silently it had drifted right underneath us and might have got into the convoy and finished my career and Bestwin's but for a happening which justifies me in saying that this is the most wonderful story of the year.

Bestwin had come on board the Dade for breakfast—the Dade was the destroyer I commanded. We exchanged notes and agreed that nothing had passed and went below to eat.

"I think she'll come by night if she comes at all," said Bestwin, "especially as the difficulty of this passage seems to be well known even in non-naval circles of Germany."

"Of course you saw nothing?" I said.

Bestwin hesitated.

"I saw nothing important," he said, "except that there seem to be a number of very large devil-fish in this quarter. I was looking over the side at four bells in the middle watch and I saw one chap as big as a table. I could see him quite plainly, all phosphorescent and hideous with his long tentacles folded behind him."

"It's rather far north for that kind of animal," I said, and we changed the subject and discussed the sort of things that men discuss at breakfast, razors and soaps, and mail and the scarcity of clean shirts.

We came on deck just as the officer of the watch hailed me.

"Something in the water ahead, sir," he said.

We made a jump for the bridge and fixed our glasses.

Sure enough something was happening. The water was swirling and foaming as though some monstrous body was in mortal agony and was threshing out its life in the depths of the sea. It was on the wrong side of the shoal—the side we didn't want to see a U-boat so that when all of a sudden a submarine broke surface my heart went down into my boots.

Bestwin took a flying leap and jumped for his boat, which was lying alongside, and the last I saw of him, his crew were pulling for their ship.

We got bear the range and opened fire.

The first shell went over, the second fell short. But what worried and puzzled me was the erratic behaviour of the U-boat. It didn't attempt to get away, but was bucking up and down for all the world like a porpoise. First the bow came out, then the stern, then it submerged altogether, and when it re-appeared it was twisting round in a circle.

I heard the gun of the Floss go and saw a column of water leap up astern of the U-boat, and then I saw it come to the level and a figure appeared on the deck waving a white flag.

It was the commander, and when he was taken off and brought to me I had never seen but one man who presented so wild and terrified an appearance. He was shaking and moaning like someone demented.

Bestwin had returned to the Dade and together we got the German down to my mess-room and forced some brandy between his chattering teeth. He looked round dazed and bewildered.

"Then it isn't a dream," he said in German.

We found afterwards that he spoke good English, and after Bestwin and I had gathered in the crew, and put some of our men aboard the submarine to bring her into harbour, and when we were through with wirelessing our report to the flagship and filling and comparing logs, we went down to see him.

He was more composed, and that was when he revealed his knowledge of the English language.

"Gentlemen," he said, "I have no doubt you have formed a very low opinion of my courage."

"Not at all," said Bestwin with innate British courtesy, "you probably thought we were going to hang you."

Kapitän-Leutnant Scholtz—for so he introduced himself—shot at George what I would describe as a look of positive dislike.

"It was not that, gentlemen," he said coldly, "no normal danger ever terrifies a German officer, but I have been through an experience which I can only describe as appalling."

He shuddered at the recollection.

"Last night," he said, "I was approaching your patrol, well knowing, of course, that a very vigilant look-out was being maintained for the protection of your transports which are now in latitude so and so, longitude so-much. I had orders, I will be perfectly frank with you, to sink the giant liner which you have stolen from my country and which carries eight thousand men of the —th U.S. Regiment of Infantry."

He had all the details pat and I don't doubt that he could have told me the birthplace of the chief steward.

"Naturally I was anxious to avoid you; but nevertheless I kept to the surface as soon as night fell and did not submerge until I was about nine nautical miles from your beat."

"To the North-west?" asked Bestwin.

"North-north-west from here," said Scholtz, and went on, "but before I submerged, and when, of course, I was in diving trim so that the boat was susceptible to the least unusual resistance, I observed I was moving in what seemed to be a veritable ocean of devil-fish."

Bestwin uttered an exclamation.

"Why, yes," he said, "I saw them myself."

"There were thousands of them," said Kapitän Scholtz with a shiver, "they lit the sea with their uncanny light. I was not greatly impressed except to find them so far north—I am something of a naturalist, particularly in relation to maricolous animals. I observed that they were rather of the order of Octopus punctatus than Octopus vulgaris, that is to say they were larger and possessed more tentacles than the European species—in fact they differed in many structural respects from the typical Cepholopoda of their order."

"I've got you," said Bestwin, who is no scientist, "they were different."

"Quite", said Scholtz; "as I say, I was not worried except in so far as the possibility with so many of these fish in the neighbourhood there was a danger that my propeller would be fouled. But really this wasn't a great danger. I was taking a final look round before submerging and my second officer had already gone below when I saw on my starboard bow what I took to be the broken mast of a ship lying in the water. I altered my course to keep it well away when, to my amazement it moved."

He wiped his brow with a handkerchief and blew as though to blow away the memory.

"It was moving broadside toward me, so that in three or four minutes I could see it plainly."

"It—then it was alive?" I asked.

"Yes," said Scholtz. "I will try to describe it. In length it was not far short of a hundred feet. It was more or less tubular in shape and the back was covered with a green mossy growth. The head, which lay flat on the water, was spatula-shaped and horny, rather like a crocodile, though as I afterwards discovered it had a huge pair of gills. It was gliding toward me without any perceptible motion. I called the second officer, but before he could reach the deck the thing had rolled over, revealing a white belly and two great fins like the centre-board of a yacht, and had disappeared. I had just time to notice what looked like a ruff of red fur about its neck, but which I afterwards discovered was a broad band of pink seaweed, Polysiphonia Urceolata."

I must confess that both Bestwin and I were staggered. Everybody has heard of the sea-serpent, the existence of which is, of course, one of the stock jokes of the world. But probably at the back of every sane man's mind there has lurked a reservation, that such animals should exist is not absolutely outside the range of possibility.

"Do you suggest," asked Bestwin, who had taken out a sheet of paper and was noting down the extraordinary facts, "that you saw the sea-serpent?"

Kapitän Scholtz shrugged his shoulders.

"What can I say?" he said, "Naturally as one interested in animals and in the sea I have heard of the sea-serpent which was seen in '48 by Captain M'Quhae in the tropic of Capricorn, and I have read Lt. Drummond's account of the monster he saw, and the description which Dr. Drevar of the Pauline furnished in '75 of the battle he had seen between a sea-serpent and a whale. Then, of course, there is the account given by the Captain of Queen Victoria's yacht Osborne, which fell in with the sea-serpent off Sicily in June 1877. I confess I am as sceptical as you, gentlemen, but there was the thing in front of my eyes. There was no question of my being under any illusion or my mistaking the animal for anything but what it was.

"However, after a little while we went below and submerged, keeping the periscope level with the water. It was not long before I picked up the destroyers. Probably my silencer accounted for the fact that you did not hear me. I had shut off and was going down a little deeper to drift under you when I saw this strange animal again. It was swimming in a wide circle and its head evidently struck against my bows, for I felt a trembling shock and we began to roll. Immediately after I felt another shock, this time against the side of the boat, and this last was so violent that I decided to come to the surface and take the chance of being observed. Accordingly I came up.

"For a little time I could see nothing, but presently right aft I discerned the head of the beast, lying across the deck, its body being under water. The head was about eleven or twelve feet long and the eyes, which turned on me and which filled me with the most awful terror, were green and luminous, like those of a crocodile. The head slid sideways toward me with such force that it swept the iron stanchions clear, and I jumped below and again submerged.

"Throughout the night I drifted aimlessly with my engines shut off, not daring, for something more than the fear of your patrol, to come to the surface, and daring as little to stay below because at odd intervals we felt the horny head of the beast striking against the boat. We had excited his curiosity and probably his anger and he kept us close company. Once he came over us and momentarily rested his weight upon the hull. I thought that our end had come. As you know, gentlemen, a submarine is so sensitively balanced that a few pounds of unexpected weight is quite sufficient to set it wobbling. Imagine what happened when two or three tons of marine monster rested on us. My bows dipped down and I should have had some difficulty in recovering, but happily the beast slipped off.

"At seven o'clock this morning I cleared the shallow water, but I had not shaken off my companion. I caught a momentary glimpse of him through my periscope, his cavernous mouth, his triple rows of teeth, his staring green eyes, but I was beginning to get used to him, and to enjoy the novel experience when something suddenly enraged him. I had risked showing my periscope and I was looking through this when the thing happened. He rose half out of the water so that the upper part of him towered over me, and then for the first time I saw that the great under-fins were working to and fro as a man might work his hands. They were for all the world like hands in fingerless mittens. The under side was covered with wide silvery scales, the fins were a dark purple and, as I say, horribly like hands. As suddenly he rose he fell again, sending up a mountainous wave. Then before I knew what had happened he had thrown himself on his back as a playful cat would lie on the ground and had seized the bottom and the sides of the boat in his terrible fins.

"The boat rolled to and fro. I could see him biting at the steel-covered bow and inside we could hear the grating of his teeth. I put on full speed and tried to sink, but the body of the creature was holding me up.

Then suddenly the stern went down and I knew, without seeing, that he had flung his tail clear of the water and had coiled it round my little boat. We rose and fell in a most alarming fashion. The crew who knew nothing of the circumstances, and the officers, to whom I had not confided my fears, could not understand what I was doing and imagined that I was manipulating the diving rudder.

"It was then that you opened fire, and I think the first shell must have wounded the beast, for he released his hold and we came up on a level bottom. Since I did not wish to share the fate of the sea-serpent," said Kapitän Scholtz with a smile, "I had nothing to do but to surrender."

We looked at one another, the three of us.

Bestwin was perhaps more excited than I.

"This is the most extraordinary thing that has ever happened," he said, "and it is quite natural in this extraordinary war, with its submarines, its depth charges and the like, that we should disturb whatever is at the bottom of the sea."

"You understand, gentlemen," interrupted Kapitän Scholtz, "and I am sure you will not take it amiss, that I myself would like to describe this event in my own way."

"In other words," said I, "you want the copyright of this story."

Kapitän Scholtz nodded. "Both the serial and the book rights," he said, and I stared at him.

"Why, Willie," I said.

He gasped. "Mr. Vanrhyn!" said he.

"Willie!" I said, "I thought you were dead, But you are alive and lying."

I shook him warmly by the hand.

"Say, Mr Vanrhyn," he said, looking mighty foolish, just as he used to when we caught him in the old Monitor-Post days. "That's a pretty good story anyway."

"Willie!" I said and introduced him.

"Scholtz is my real name," he explained, "Mainz was my nom de plume, and I got the idea for that story," he said, "by seeing all those devil fish—and Mr.Vanrhyn," he said earnestly, "I wanted some story bad. That old transport is full of Chicago boys, half of 'em friends of mine. It was a question," he said, "of thinking or sinking, and I had to think up an excuse for surrendering pretty quick or my second officer would have shot me. I got all my facts and Latin words out of an encyclopedia I looted. How does the story go?"

"Willie," I said, "that sea-serpent copyright is yours for all time. I'll file it just as soon as I get back to New York."

Edgar Wallace – A Short Biography

Richard Horatio Edgar Wallace was born on the 1st April 1875 at 7 Ashburnham Grove, Greenwich. His mother, Mary Jane "Polly" Richards was born into an Irish Catholic family in Liverpool in 1843 and had worked in theatres, both as an actress in bit-parts and as a stagehand and usherette, until she married a Merchant Navy Captain, Joseph Richards, in 1867. He too had been born into an Irish Catholic family in Liverpool. His father had also been a Captain in the Merchant Navy, and his mother's family had a marine background. Mary was eight months pregnant with Joseph's child when he died at sea, and it was once the child had been born that she first turned to the stage, taking the stage name Polly Richards.

She joined the Marriott family theatre troupe in 1872. It was managed by Mrs. Alice Edgar, Richard Edgar, Grace Edgar, Adeline Edgar and Richard Horatio Edgar, Wallace's father. In late 1874 Mary and Richard Horatio Edgar had a brief sexual encounter at the party following a successful show, and she fell pregnant. Worried about the scandal which would ensue and fearing that she might forever lose her job at the troupe, she fabricated an obligation in Greenwich would detain her there for at least six months. She lived in a room in the boarding house on Ashburnham Grove until her son, Edgar, was born. She had already made preparations through her midwife for a couple to foster the child, and when Edgar was born the midwife presented her with Mrs Freeman. Her husband was a fishmonger at Billingsgate market and she already had ten children. She was happy to foster the child and for Polly to make frequent visits to see him in exchange for a small sum of money which Polly made from her work in the theatre troupe.

Wallace was now known as Richard Horatio Edgar Freeman, taking his father's forenames and his foster family's surname. Broadly speaking his childhood was a happy one. The Freemans looked after him lovingly and he had good friendships with his foster siblings, particularly Clara Freeman, twenty years his senior, who often looked after him as a child. After a few years Polly's finances tightened and she was no longer in a position to afford the fee she had been paying the Freemans. However, they had grown to love the young Wallace and opted to adopt him in order to keep him out of the workhouse. Polly could no longer visit him. George Freeman was keen to ensure that he had equal opportunities and did all he could to secure him an education at St. Alfege with St. Peter's, a Peckham boarding school. Despite his adoptive father's efforts, though, Wallace left the school aged twelve for truancy.

Instead he went to work and by the time he was fourteen or fifteen he had experience selling newspapers at Ludgate Circus, near Fleet Street, as a worker in a rubber factory, as a shoe shop assistant, as a milk delivery boy and as a ship's cook. He stole from the milk company which resulted in his dismissal, and in 1894 was engaged to a local girl from Deptford named Edith Anstree, though he broke this off and instead joined the Infantry. He adopted the name Edgar Wallace which he took from Lew Wallace, the author of *Ben-Hur*, and his medical record records a diminutive 33" chest and a stunted growth. his first posting was with the West Kent Regiment in South Africa in 1896, though he did not enjoy military life, arranging to be transferred to the Royal Army Medical Corps. Though this was a less strenuous job, it was also significantly less pleasant and so he again transferred to the Press Corps, which he found suited him far better.

He was in Cape Town in 1898 where he met Rudyard Kipling and was inspired to begin writing and publishing poetry and songs. His first collection of ballads, *The Mission that Failed!* and was enough of a success that in 1899 he paid his way out of the armed forces in order to turn to writing full time. His first work was as a war correspondent for Reuters who kept him in Africa to cover the Boer War, and then for the Daily Mail in 1900 and various other periodicals after that. It was while he was in South Africa that he met and married Ivy Maude Caldecott, who was 21 when they married in 1901, despite her

Wesleyan missionary father's strong opposition to the union, for several reasons, one of which was that Wallace's writing was not turning quite the profit he had expected it would. *War and Other Poems* and *Writ in Barracks,* both published in 1900, had not proved as popular as his first collection. Eleanor Clare Hellier Wallace, their first child, died of meningitis in 1903 and, in rather deep debt, they returned to London. Wallace used his contacts with the Daily Mail to get work with them in London, electing to write detective novels as a means of making quick money.

Wallace met Polly, his birth mother, in 1903. He didn't remember her from his childhood as he had been too young when she became unable to visit, so it was as though they were meeting for the first time. She was sixty years old and terminally ill, living in abject poverty. She had come to Wallace seeking financial support, but he turned her away. She died in the Bradford Infirmary later that year. In 1904 he and Ivy had a son, Bryan. He was still writing and had completed his first thriller, *The Four Just Men*. Since nobody would publish it he resorted to setting up his own publishing company which he called Tallis Press and he published a serialised version of *The Four Just Men* in 1905. He received promotional assistance from the Daily Mail in which he ran a competition for entrants to guess the method of murder in the final chapter, with a prize of £1,000 for a correct guess. Although the paper's proprietor, Lord Alfred Harmsworth, refused Wallace the £1,000 prize money, Wallace persisted and went ahead with the competition, recklessly advertising on billboards and buses all over the country, hoping to expand his advertisements across the Empire. His worried colleagues at the Daily Mail managed to convince him to lower the prize money to £500, split into a first prize of £250, a second prize of £200 and a third of £50, but with the total cost of his advertisements nearing £2,000 he would need to sell £2,500 worth of copies before he could see any profit. He was confident that this could be achieved in just three months.

Though he had remarkable enthusiasm, it became clear that his managerial skills left a lot to be desired. It soon emerged that nowhere in the competition terms and conditions had he included a clause limiting the competition to one single winner; instead, any entrant with a winning answer was entitled to their corresponding prize money. Thus, if ten entrants guessed the first prize answer, the competition was obliged to pay each entrant £250. This error was only noticed after the competition had been closed and the solution had been printed in the final installment of the novel, meaning that not only was there no opportunity to write his way out of enormous financial obligation, but the entrants who had guessed correctly would by now have read the final chapter and know they had done so. £250 was an enormous amount of money to the average Edwardian family and those entitled to it were likely to make a lot of noise if they didn't receive their money. Despite this, Wallace's fist instinct was to attempt to ignore the issue entirely, even as he discovered that he initial calculations had been dramatically over-enthusiastic and it would take nearer to two years of continuous sales to break even at the initial cost of £2,500, let alone the new figure which included every correct guesser. Compounding the problem even further was the awful realisation that as sales continued throughout the initial three month period and Wallace approached the £2,500 break-even figure, new readers were still eligible to enter and guess correctly. Though it is unknown how much he eventually owed his readers, Lord Harmsworth found himself having to loan over £5,000 in order to protect the reputation of the newspaper, since 1906 had come around and there still hadn't been a list printed of all prize-winners. It was less a charitable act than one of a man anxious that the failure would reflect ill on his own paper. Wallace filed for bankruptcy shortly thereafter and as a token gesture to his creditors sold the rights to the novel to Sir George Newnes, a publisher and editor, for £75. In the midst of this chaos though, Wallace managed to write and published *Smithy*, which would become the first of a series of *Smithy* novels.

Following this fiascos Wallace was dismissed from the Daily Mail in 1907 when inaccuracies which were found in his reporting, resulting in libel cases being brought against the paper. That year he became the first reporter to be fired from the Daily Mail and was his awful reputation prevented him from finding work at any other papers. Despite all this, though, he travelled to the Congo Free State later that year and reported on the criminal treatment of the Congolese people by King Leopold II of Belgium and the Belgian rubber companies. Up to fifteen million Congolese were killed in various atrocities, and Wallace was asked to serialise stories based on his experiences for her penny magazine *Weekly Tale-Teller*. He and Ivy had another daughter, named Patricia, in 1908. Though his new work for *Weekly Tale-Teller* was bringing in some money, their financial situation was still dire and Ivy was occasionally forced to sell off her jewellery and possessions in order to pay for food. In 1911 his Congolese stories were published in a collection called *Sanders of the River*, which quickly became a bestseller. He would publish eleven more such collections featuring a total of 102 stories of adventure and tribal life set on the river Congo.

From 1908 he started to enjoy a revival of both his success and his reputation. The majority of his initial writing he sold outright in order to make money as quickly as possible and placate his creditors in the United Kingdom and South Africa, but as his success saw the reestablishment of his reputation he began to find work once again as a journalist, beginning in horse racing for the *Week-End*, the *Evening News* and then as an editor for the *Week-End Racing Supplement*. Following this success he started his own racing papers, *Bibury's* and *R. E. Walton's Weekly*, eventually buying his own racehorses and losing thousands gambling. His success was insufficient to support his newly extravagant lifestyle and his marriage began to fail in the light of his financial irresponsibility. He and Ivy had their last child together, Michael Blair Wallace, in 1916, and she filed for divorce in 1918 moving to Tunbridge Wells with her children.

Wallace began to fall for his secretary Ethel Violet King and they married in 1921, having a child, Penelope Wallace, in 1923, who would herself go on to become a successful crime writer. Wallace now began to take his career as a fiction writer more seriously, signing with Hodder and Stoughton in 1921. He now began to organize his contracts more carefully, arranging for royalties and properly organized promotions, run by people more business-minded than himself. He was marketed as the 'King of Thrillers' and they gave him the trademark image of a trilby, a cigarette holder and a yellow Rolls Royce. He was truly prolific, capable not only of producing a 70,000 word novel in three days but of doing three novels in a row in such a manner. His publishers signed off on almost everything he wrote as soon as he turned it in, estimating that by 1928 one in four books being read at any time was written by Wallace, for alongside his famous thrillers he wrote variously in other genres, including but not limited to science fiction, non-fiction accounts of WWI which amounted to ten volumes and screen plays. Eventually he would reach the remarkable total of 170 novels, 18 stage plays and 957 short stories.

Wallace became chairman of the Press Club which to this day holds an annual Edgar Wallace Award, rewarding 'excellence in writing'. In 1923 he broadcasted a report on the Epsom Derby horse race for the British Broadcasting Company, making him the first ever radio sports correspondent. His ex-wife Ivy had suffered from breast cancer between 1923-1924, and it eventually killed her in 1926 despite a successful operation to remove a tumour the year before. He wrote the essay "The Canker in our Midst" in 1926 which dealt, aggressively and controversially, with the problem of paedophilia in show business, describing how children were unwittingly left open to sexual abuse, and linking paedophilia with homosexuality. Its tone has been described as "intolerant, blustering, kick-the-blighters-down-the-stairs". He was appointed chairman of the British Lion Film Corporation on the back of the success of *The Ringer* and on the agreement that he give British Lion first choice on all his future work. This contract gave him an annual salary and a large amount of stock with the company, along with a stipend on all British Lion production of his work and 10% of their annual profits. This extraordinary contract gave him annual earnings by 1929 of almost £50,000, or almost £2 million in 2014.

He now became an active figure in politics, entering the 1931 general election as a Liberal contestant in Blackpool, rejecting the current government in favour of free trade. He lost the election by over 33,000 votes and went to America in late 1931, once again deeply in debt after buying the *Sunday News* which closed six months later. In America he quickly found work as a script doctor for RKO Pictures, enjoying early success with the 1932 adaptation of *The Hound of the Baskervilles*. This success, along with that of the play *The Green Pack*, established his reputation in America and he was able to see his own work adapted for film, beginning with *The Four Just Men*. His most successful theatrical work, *On The Spot*, which explores the life of Al Capone, has been described as "arguably, in construction, dialogue, action, plot and resolution, still one of the finest and purest of 20th-century melodramas". These successes led to his assignation on RKO's "gorilla picture" which would become famous as King Kong in 1933.

He worked on the first draft though he was beginning to experience severe headaches which brought about a diagnosis of diabetes. Despite taking medication to address his condition, it deteriorated in a matter of days. His wife booked him passage home but soon heard that he had entered a coma and died of his condition and double pneumonia on the 7th of February 1932 in North Maple Drive, Beverly Hills. In his honour the bell at St. Bride's church on Fleet Street tolled for the duration of the morning while the flags flew at half-mast. He was buried near his home in England at Chalklands, Bourne End, in Buckinghamshire. Once again, at the time of his death he was in severe debt, mostly to racing bookkeepers, though these debts were settled within two years thanks to the enormous royalties his estate continued to receive from his contracts. His writing has been translated into 29 languages, and is considered one of the most important bodies of Colonial writing.

Edgar Wallace – A Concise Bibliography

African Novels
Sanders of the River (1911)
The People of the River (1911)
The River of Stars (1913)
Bosambo of the River (1914)
Bones (1915)
The Keepers of the King's Peace (1917)
Lieutenant Bones (1918)
Bones in London (1921)
Sandi the Kingmaker (1922)
Bones of the River (1923)
Sanders (1926)
Again Sanders (1928)

Four Just Men (Series)
The Four Just Men (1905)
The Council of Justice (1908)
The Just Men of Cordova (1917)
The Law of the Four Just Men (US title: Again the Three Just Men) (1921)
The Three Just Men (1926)
Again the Three Just Men (US title: The Law of the Three Just Men) (1929) a.k.a. Again the Three

Captains of Souls (1923)
The Clue of the New Pin (1923)
The Green Archer (1923)
The Missing Million (1923)
The Dark Eyes of London or The Croakers (1924)
Double Dan or Diana of Kara-Kara (US Title) (1924)
The Face in the Night or The Diamond Men or The Ragged Princess (1924)
The Sinister Man (1924)
The Three Oak Mystery (1924)
The Blue Hand or Beyond Recall (1925)
The Daughters of the Night (1925)
The Gaunt Stranger or Police Work (1925) revised as The Ringer (1926)
A King by Night (1925)
The Strange Countess (1925)
The Avenger or The Hairy Arm (1926)
The Black Abbot (1926)
The Day of Uniting (1926)
The Door with Seven Locks (1926)
The Man from Morocco or Souls In Shadows or The Black (US Title) (1926)
The Million Dollar Story (1926)
The Northing Tramp or The Tramp (1926)
Penelope of the Polyantha (1926)
The Square Emerald or The Woman (1926)
The Terrible People or The Gallows' Hand (1926)
We Shall See! or The Gaol-Breakers (US Title) (1926)
The Yellow Snake or The Black Tenth (1926)
Big Foot (1927)
The Feathered Serpent or Inspector Wade or Inspector Wade and the Feathered Serpent (1927)
Flat 2 (1927)
The Forger or The Counterfeiter (1927)
Terror Keep (1927)
The Hand of Power or The Proud Sons of Ragusa (1927)
The Man Who Was Nobody (1927)
Number Six (1927)
The Squeaker or The Sign of the Leopard or The Squealer (US Title) (1927)
The Traitor's Gate (1927)
The Double (1928)
The Flying Squad (1928)
The Gunner or Gunman's Bluff (US Title) (1928)
Four Square Jane or The Fourth Square (1929)
The Golden Hades or Stamped In Gold or The Sinister Yellow Sign (1929)
The Green Ribbon (1929)
The Calendar (1930)
The Clue of the Silver Key or The Silver Key (1930)
The Lady of Ascot (1930)
The Devil Man or Sinister Street or Silver Steel
or The Life and Death of Charles Peace (1931)
The Man at the Carlton or The Mystery of Mary Grier (1931)

The Coat of Arms or The Arranways Mystery (1931)
On the Spot: Violence and Murder in Chicago (1931)
When the Gangs Came to London or Scotland Yard's Yankee Dick
or The Gangsters Come To London (1932)
The Frightened Lady or The Case of the Frightened Lady or Criminal At Large (1933)
The Green Pack (1933)
The Man Who Changed His Name (1935)
The Mouthpiece (1935)
Smoky Cell (1935)
The Table (1936)
Sanctuary Island (1936)

Other Novels

Captain Tatham of Tatham Island or Eve's Island or The Island of Galloping Gold (1909)
The Duke in the Suburbs (1909)
Private Selby (1912)
1925 - The Story of a Fatal Peace (1915)
Those Folk of Bulboro (1918)
The Book of all Power (1921)
Flying Fifty-five (1922)
The Books of Bart (1923)
Barbara on Her Own (1926)

Poetry Collections

The Mission That Failed (1898)
War and Other Poems (1900)
Writ In Barracks (1900)

Non-Fiction

Unofficial Despatches of the Anglo-Boer War (1901)
Famous Scottish Regiments (1914)
Field Marshal Sir John French (1914)
Heroes All: Gallant Deeds of the War (1914)
The Standard History of the War – Volumes 1 – 4 (1914)
Kitchener's Army and the Territorial Forces:
The Full Story of a Great Achievement (1915)
Vol. 2-4. War of the Nations (1915)
Vol. 5-7. War of the Nations (1916)
Vol. 8-9. War of the Nations (1917)
Famous Men and Battles of the British Empire (1917)
Tam of the Scouts (1918)
The Real Shell-Man: The Story of Chetwynd of Chilwell (1919)
People or Edgar Wallace by Himself (1926)
The Trial of Patrick Herbert Mahon (1928)
My Hollywood Diary (1932)

Screenplays

King Kong (1932, first draft of original screenplay, 110 pages) While the script was not used in its entirety, much of it was retained for the final screenplay.
The Hound of the Baskervilles (1932, British film)
The Squeaker (1930, British film)
Prince Gabby (1929, British film)
Mark of the Frog (1928, American film)
The Valley of Ghosts (192

The Admirable Carfew (1914)
The Adventure of Heine (1917)
Tam O' the Scouts (1918)
The Fighting Scouts (1919)
Chick (1923)
The Black Avons (1925)
The Brigand (1927)
The Mixer (1927)
This England (1927)
The Orator (1928)
The Thief in the Night (1928)
Elegant Edward (1928)
The Lone House Mystery and Other Stories (1929)
The Governor of Chi-Foo (1929)
Again the Ringer The Ringer Returns (US Title) (1929)
The Big Four or Crooks of Society (1929)
The Black or Blackmailers I Have Foiled (1929)
The Cat-Burglar (1929)
Circumstantial Evidence (1929)
Fighting Snub Reilly (1929)
For Information Received (1929)
Forty-Eight Short Stories (1929)
Planetoid 127 and The Sweizer Pump (1929)
The Ghost of Down Hill & The Queen of Sheba's Belt (1929)
The Iron Grip (1929)
The Lady of Little Hell (1929)
The Little Green Man (1929)
The Prison-Breakers (1929)
The Reporter (1929)
Killer Kay (1930)
Mrs William Jones and Bill (1930)
Forty Eight Short Stories (George Newnes Limited ca. 1930)
The Stretelli Case and Other Mystery Stories (1930)
The Terror (1930)
The Lady Called Nita (1930)
Sergeant Sir Peter or Sergeant Dunn, C.I.D. (1932)
The Scotland Yard Book of Edgar Wallace (1932)
The Steward (1932)
Nig-Nog and other humorous stories (1934)

The Last Adventure (1934)
The Woman From the East (1934) Co-written By Robert George Curtis
The Edgar Wallace Reader of Mystery and Adventure (1943)
The Undisclosed Client (1963)

Other

King Kong, with Draycott M. Dell, (1933), 28 October 1933 Cinema Weekly

Plays

An African Millionaire (1904)
The Forest of Happy Dreams (1910)
Dolly Cutting Herself (1911)
The Manager's Dream (1914)
M'Lady (1921)
Double Dan (1926)
The Mystery of room 45 (1926)
A Perfect Gentleman (1927)
The Terror (1927)
Traitors Gate (1927)
The Lad (1928)
The Man Who Changed His Name (1928)
The Squeaker (1928)
The Calendar (1929)
Persons Unknown (1929)
The Ringer (1929)
The Mouthpiece (1930)
On the Spot (1930)
Smoky Cell (1930)
The Squeaker (1930)
To Oblige A Lady (1930)
The Case of the Frightened Lady (1931)
The Old Man (1931)
The Green Pack (1932)
The Table (1932)